"I Can't Just Move Into Your Home To Stay, Hunter."

"Why not, Beth? I spend most of my evenings and nights in the studio, anyway. Stay here. Put down roots. When your ex-husband appears, if he does, face him from within the fortress of a stable life. Security and stability can be powerful weapons."

"Security and stability?"

"It's called *home,* Beth."

Her protest died on her tongue. To some, Hunter was the elusive artist. To others, a brutal half-breed. To Beth, the man who knelt at her feet was a gentle knight in faded denim. He offered the gift of her dreams. Dignity and peace and sweet, mysterious magic. "I don't want you to be hurt," she whispered to him. "Not any more. Not by anyone."

"Some things are worth the risk," he responded.

"Yes," she said and knew it was true.

"Then you'll stay. This will be the end of your journey. For a while."

"I'll stay," she answered. "We'll take the risks and explore this magic, and when it's time, I'll go."

Dear Reader:

Welcome to Silhouette Desire! What a month this is, with six sinfully sexy heroes from six sensational countries featured in our *Man of the World* program. You'll be finding out all about these tantalizing men between the covers of six romances written by some of your favorite authors: Linda Lael Miller, Lucy Gordon, Kathleen Korbel, Barbara Faith, Jennifer Greene, and BJ James.

By now I'm sure you've noticed the portraits of our heroes on the covers of each *Man of the World* book. Aren't these hunks handsome? I simply couldn't decide which hero I loved the best, so I decided to just love them all.

And don't miss the special letter from the author in front of each book. These talented women have taken a little extra time to compose some words to you, describing how they chose their hero and his country.

So thrill to the sensuous love stories in *Men of the World*. From the United States to Europe to the hot desert sands, the books are about six heroes you'll never forget. Please don't hesitate to write and tell me what you think of this exciting program *and* of Silhouette Desire. I'm always more than happy to hear from our readers.

I know you'll love *Men of the World*. Happy reading!

Lucia Macro

Senior Editor

BJ
JAMES

SLADE'S WOMAN

SILHOUETTE *Desire*

Published by Silhouette Books New York

America's Publisher of Contemporary Romance

SILHOUETTE BOOKS
300 East 42nd St., New York, N.Y. 10017

SLADE'S WOMAN

ISBN: 0-373-05672-9

First Silhouette Books printing October 1991

Printed in the U.S.A.

BJ JAMES

married her high school sweetheart straight out of college and soon found that books were delightful companions during her lonely nights as a doctor's wife. Her life is filled with her loving husband and family, pets, writing . . . and romance.

A Special Letter From BJ James

Dear Reader:

The thought that I should write did not spring from discontent nor disenchantment. No book was flung aside with the declaration that I could do better. For every book that did not enchant, there was always one whose story was magic. Yet in the changing roles of my life—from rowdy tomboy to mother of three sons—I never envisioned being more than a reader. I never expected to be among the blessed, letting my imagination soar, weaving magic of my own. Until one day, a friend—a bookseller, a writer— dared me to write. The rowdy tomboy, who survives still, has *never* refused a dare.

It was a beginning. Dreams I dared not dream have come true. Now books are more than companions. They are my creation, as well. Silhouette Desire affords the freedom to create, to write drama as well as passion, to paint with words a mood, an ambience, making it an integral force, to write with the intensity that has become my trademark. Writing the male point of view for *Man of the Month* adds yet another dimension. Within its broad scope, contrasts are more powerfully drawn, passion made more exquisite. Characters become stronger, more human. The mystery is not lost when we feel a lover's pain, or know his joy. He only becomes more unforgettable.

Why for the *Men of the World* program did I choose America? The answer is simple. From the wild and gentle shores of the Atlantic, over mountains majestic and stark, through shadowed canyons and windswept deserts, to the untamed Pacific beyond, what country is as breathtaking, as exciting? And like his country, what man is tougher, more tender, more intriguing, more exasperating . . . or more wonderful than the American Male? Who better represents the blend of our pioneer heritage than the son of a native American—a Cherokee—and an English adventurer?

Hunter Slade of *Slade's Woman*—half-breed, tough, tender. The American Man! I hope you fall in love with him.

Sincerely,

BJ James

Prologue

Hunter Slade looked down at the sketch pad in his hand. The face captured there by broad strokes and delicate shadings was not the usual dark, coppery coloring of the Cherokee. Instead, the pale skin, the tangle of tawny gold hair, the gentle features were pure Anglo-Saxon. He added another line, and the perfect, smiling mouth with lips like a dewy rose held a secret sadness.

"Yes," he said softly, and wondered again, as he had for most of his life, what quirk of nature allowed him to see the random lines and strokes that created her lovely face but turned the printed word to a maddening jumble. Restlessly, he put the pad aside. Not because he was displeased with his work. But because he had captured too well the quiet dignity, the gentle need beneath the smile, the haunting fear and sadness.

Rising, he cast a glance at the gathering of silent figures of terra-cotta and sculptor's stone, who watched and waited for his hand. Soon, they would begin the journey down the mountain to the coast. There, at the museum in Brighton, under the guardianship of Marlee Adamson, septuagenarian, friend, mentor, they would become part of the most important showing of his work. The larger pieces of bronze and stone had already gone. But these tiny and fragile ones, his favorites, he would pack himself.

But not yet. They required the greatest concentration, and his mind was not at ease. There was a turbulence in him that made his hand impatient and unsure. A disquiet that tensed his massive shoulders and knotted his gut. The restlessness gathering like a storm drove him to his feet. The walls were closing in. He wondered briefly if this was what it was like to be a caged panther. Padding, padding, with something akin to rage building like a volcano. He smiled wryly. At least a panther had enough sense not to live in a cage of his own making.

Flexing shoulders that were broad even for a man of six feet five inches, he turned away from the studio. Beyond the open doors, the mountains beckoned. His steps were silent on the rough-hewn stone of the terrace floor. Above the studio, higher on the mountain, his mountain, in a blend of stone, weathered wood and glass, lay his home. Beyond the terrace railing lay his land.

Within his view of the sprawling, distant Appalachians lay the Great Smokies, a national park that belonged to no man, yet was every man's land. In Hunter's heart—where to have something meant to love it, not possess it—each mountain rising against the horizon, each valley nestled in their shadows, was his. He loved the sea, the tidelands and the savannahs, but here, in this special place the Cherokee called the land of a thousand smokes, he was home.

In these ruffled hills that seemed to reach to the sky, he found patience. In the magic of the blue mists, he found

tranquillity. In forest sounds, magnified by silence, there
was harmony. In the moist fragrance of growing things there
was rebirth of the spirit. In the dignity of monoliths, sanded
and torn by wind and water for over two hundred million
years, he found his own. The solitude of these tall guardi-
ans was his. They always soothed him. But not now.

"Don't be a fool, Slade." His voice was a hollow echo in
the stillness. Though he tried to heed his own advice and lose
himself in the magnificence of the golden candlelight of
sunset, he found no escape from her.

The sky became a canvas and on it, his eyes drew her face.
The blue on the horizon was the blue of her eyes. The candlelight, the tawny flush of her cheeks. The shifting clouds,
the fleeting shadow of hidden sadness.

His hands closed into fists. His wild mane of coal black
hair was flung back from his face. Obsidian eyes glittered.
This had happened only once before, this compelling attraction to a face, a smile, the lush womanly grace. Only
once.

There had been women in Hunter's life, transient women,
part of the rebellion of a wild, half-savage youth. Later,
when the direction of his life changed, there were women
like himself, who never let down their guard, never opened
the door to their hearts, women who wanted only the excitement of a moment. Perhaps they shared a moment to
remember, perhaps not, but it was never more. Then one
woman, sophisticated, worldly, with hair as black as his own
and eyes like coal, shattered the wall he had built about his
young heart. She teased and enticed and beguiled, wrapping herself around him until the part of him that wanted
and needed to love succumbed to her. Then as abruptly as
it began, the game was over. The aloof and elusive Hunter
was only a scalp for her belt. Love was an encumbrance,

worthless booty to be discarded along the way to fame and success.

She was the first woman to haunt his thoughts and his dreams. And, after a lesson well learned, she was the last. Walls rebuilt by pain became impenetrable. His will was iron, his heart was stone. No woman had touched him. Until now.

"No!" The face he'd drawn belonged to a stranger, and like the blue mists, she would pass through his life without speaking, without touching. It was only the oppressive heat, the seething turbulence of clouds, fiery from the setting sun, that set him on edge. It was his sixth sense warning of change that turned his thoughts restive and honed his body to a fever pitch. Only that.

He needed no stranger in his life, no golden-haired woman with a hurt smile.

Even as he vowed there would not be, she was there in his memory, all tousled and golden, smiling that sweet, aching smile. He drew a deep, rasping breath that ended in a groan. His hand crashed down on the stone rail. His body shuddered. With an expletive as Anglo-Saxon as her face, he turned away.

As he strode with an angry step through the studio, a voice from the past mocked him, asking, *Where are you going, Hunter Slade?*

"To her," he snarled like a panther to the mountains, to the silent waiting figures, to himself. "Like a fool."

One

Fog descended on the tiny village of Sunshine, creeping past shuttered shops and empty buildings, twining catlike and lazy about glimmering street lamps. It drifted through hedgerows and trees, over houses and lawns. Then, in pale, cooling tendrils, it slid through the darkness of dusty roads, thickening, deepening, obscuring. At last, it reached a building set apart from the others, cloaking even the garish neon of Bert's Diner in a mist of red.

Inside the diner, Beth Warren paused in her work. Forgetting the cluttered table she was clearing, she stared out at the night. Hot and weary from her labor, she longed for its refuge. The irony of her wish for cool darkness brought a wry smile to her lips. She'd come to the village only a week ago. A destination randomly chosen for its isolation, the meager cost of a bus ticket and the illusion of its name.

Sunshine. Balm for the wounds of a marriage gone awry. Warmth for the void of a barren life.

A coin rattled; the jukebox blared. A primitive beat thundered in her head, the keening of a sitar skittered down the ragged edge of frayed nerves. Beth turned from the cool invitation of the window to the glare of the nearly deserted diner. Heat, light, the odor of food sickened her. It was past midnight; only two customers remained. Soon, she could close up and go home.

"Hey, baby, let's dance."

The command slithered about her like an oily tentacle, sliding through the frenzied rhythm, tainting her with its ugly intent. A man in his early twenties with a pretty, petulant face rose from his seat. His pale, cunning eyes raked over her, plundering boldly the thrust of her full breasts, lingering brazenly on the long, slender curve of her thighs. Quiet revulsion shuddered through her, and with it, relief.

For more than an hour, stripped and defiled by those watching eyes she had waited for the inevitable. With the sneering wheedle, the waiting ended. There was a small comfort in that—better to face the situation than cringe under a cloud of brewing trouble. She'd learned this lesson well, if too late.

With a mental shrug, she repulsed an intrusive thought. The past was done and beyond changing, no matter how she might wish to. This graceless young man was the present.

Beth's gaze flicked past him to the third occupant of the diner. A dark man, older than her would-be suitor, interested only in the steaming cup that rested in the curl of his hands. He had not looked up at the churlish demand. No help there, but she wasn't seeking any. In the chaotic years of her marriage to Eric Weston, and in the months since its dissolution, she'd become expert at parrying advances more dangerous and insistent than this crude gambit.

"Wanna dance and you're the only one available." The wavering whine slid into a hiccuping giggle. "Unless I dance with the breed. Breeds do dance, don't they, Slade?"

The contempt in the unsteady falsetto caught her, sending a note of warning. She realized she'd been staring blindly past the callow man who stood before her. Her attention returned to his leering face, the jerky swaying of his body, the obscene thrusting of his hips. And, with a sense of foreboding, on the negligent hand gesturing toward the solitary diner who watched them now with a dispassionate smile that left his black eyes untouched.

"C'mere, honey." The younger man smirked confidently, his lightless eyes flicked over her in avid hunger. His rhythmic sway became a preening swagger and Beth knew she'd made a mistake. This miscreant, strutting like a handsome rooster, interpreted her distraction as uncertainty or, in arrogance, a coy invitation.

"No, I'm sorry." She tempered the rejection as much as she could, mindful of the danger in hurt pride. "It's closing time."

"So? You close later." He twisted his shoulders to the beat and moved a step closer. His hand darted out to curve about her waist, manicured nails biting into her flesh.

"No!" This time, she was firmer, leaving no room for doubt as she dodged from his grasp. His smirk faded. Deep within dull eyes fluttered something cruel and ugly.

The pounding music stopped. In the merciful lull, she heard only the heave of his angry breath. He was so close, it brushed her cheek with the fetid reek of alcohol. Struggling to hide her disgust, she challenged him stare for stare. She held her ground, certain that any show of fear or weakness would be disastrous.

The jukebox whirred, another record fell into place. Then in the instant before another blaring tune could begin, a soft voice intruded.

"Miss?" The single word was pleasantly resonant. "A refill, please."

Thankful for the diversion, Beth sidestepped the leering youth, swept up the coffeepot and moved to the booth where the soft-spoken customer waited. In the week she'd worked in the diner, this dark, silent man had come in twice. He always sat in a booth near the door, never so much as glanced at the menu, drank only coffee, spoke little and tipped generously when he left. Though she'd been acutely aware of his massive size, his ruggedly handsome features and his brooding silence, she'd treated him with the same courteous reserve as her other customers. Tonight, as she filled his cup, she noted that even as he sat, his head was hardly lower than her own. His shoulders were wide, the skin pulled taut over high cheekbones was tanned. Rare silver threaded sparingly through the shaggy black of his hair.

She hadn't given it a thought for such things did not matter to her, but the younger man's slur made her realize that this man did have the strong, handsome coloring of an American Indian. It still did not matter; she was simply grateful. Softly, at his shoulder, she murmured, "Thank you."

He nodded curtly, and Beth was surprised by a leap of disappointment. She wanted to hear him speak in that slow, easy drawl that was a soothing current amid troubled waters. A fanciful illusion! He'd done no more than ask for coffee. Then with his silence, he dismissed her, untangling himself from her sordid little drama. Perhaps he assumed as others had that her reluctance was meant to be overcome.

Music, for once quietly begun, escalated to a skull-rattling volume and Beth turned away. Her sigh was lost in its boom.

This brooding stranger wouldn't be the first to assume the advances were not unwelcome. It hadn't mattered before. This time, for reasons she couldn't begin to fathom, it did.

"I must be mad!" she muttered. What else would prompt her to stand in a shabby diner worrying about the good opinion of a man she had seen only twice before and might never see again? "Only madness," she muttered again. Bracing herself, she hurried past the booth where the younger man sat hunched over his table. Any hope that his interest had cooled was destroyed when his arm flashed out, hooking about her waist with the speed of a striking snake. There was tempered steel in his hands as he drew her roughly to his table.

"Let me go," she said evenly, paying no heed to the coffee that spattered over her wrist.

"You know that's not what you want, sugar."

Fighting a rush of anger, she stood in the prison of his arms. Refusing him the satisfaction of a struggle, she ignored the splayed fingers that moved provocatively over her midriff. "You've had your fun, now, let me go."

His high-pitched giggle, mindless and irrational, destroyed any hope of a graceful escape. "You don't wanna dance—" he drew her closer, nearly dragging her down over him "—then how about a little service?"

"You've had enough beer," she said tightly. Only one here, but how many before? she wondered. How much alcoholic courage had it taken to end the siege of staring?

"Who said anything about beer?" His breath was hot and wet on her face. "You know what I want." He giggled again, and his fingers coiled about her breast.

Coolly and deliberately, without a second of hesitation, Beth poured the last of the steaming coffee in his lap.

For a stunned instant, he only stared up at her. Then in slow motion, he looked mutely down at the brown stain spreading over his groin. Then he screamed. A howl of agony tore from him like the cry of a rabid animal. Wildly, he flung her away, slamming her against the counter, shattering the empty pot. With a crash, he upended the table. Fueled by pain and rage, his strength was inhuman, his speed unbelievable. Fingers clutched her throat, digging, squeezing, no longer coiling. His whimpering moans became a demented paroxysm of the frantic rhythm of the music. With her last conscious thought, Beth saw true madness in his feral face. Then silence exploded in her head and darkness embraced her.

The floor was hard and cool. Glass pricked at her shoulder, her mind clawed at her, her face hurt, her thoughts rambled. She longed to slide back into oblivion. Yet she knew she mustn't. Struggling to sit erect, she forced open eyelids weighted by thick tears. Wiping them away with the back of her hand, she tried to focus, but fog had stolen past the window, filling the diner with its white illusion. Pain stabbed at her side like a jagged knife, and she remembered.

No music bleated at her, no mad eyes glared, no fingers crushed her throat. A terrible, waiting hush filled the diner, and one voice rippled through the stillness.

"Sunshine's little Billy Archer, back from the big city and nothing's changed. You still like to hurt smaller people, don't you? Why not me, Billy-boy? Size shouldn't matter. You're tough, remember? You just proved it." Despite the fearsome threat running through it, the voice was resonant and beautiful. A sorcerer's chant coaxing the foolhardy to retribution. Beth shuddered even as she felt its magic.

As her vision and her thoughts began to clear, she realized her assailant still crouched above her, frozen in an attitude of waiting. The telltale stain darkening the crotch of his tight jeans served as an unneeded reminder. She searched for a name. *Archer.* She'd heard the beautiful voice call him Archer.

Beyond him, with the cord of the silent jukebox dangling over his hand, stood the dark man. Slade? She searched her fuzzy memory. Yes. It was Slade speaking in hypnotic rhythm. A husky half whisper, more commanding than a shout, as seductive as it was dangerous.

Listening to him, Beth felt the irrational urge to scream at Archer, to warn him that he must run. She wanted to run herself. As she sank back to the floor, exhausted with her efforts, she wondered if she could force her tired limbs to obey, would she run from Slade or to him? She had no answer, and as the fog gathered again, she forgot the question.

In a dream, she heard their voices. Slade's, an unhurried melody. Archer's, a frightened screech of pain and bravado. Trapped in her little vacuum, she was a captive audience.

"Come on, little man, come on."

"Stay out of this, Slade. It's not your business."

"Part of this little performance was for me, wasn't it? That makes it my my business."

"You don't scare me. You won't hit me. You're afraid to."

"Am I?"

"You'll go to jail like before if you do."

"Will I?"

"Cherokee breed! Dummy!"

"Dummy, Billy? Have you forgotten the last man who called me that didn't call anybody anything for a long time?"

"You don't scare me."

"Don't I?"

"No!" The word slid into a scream.

"You lie, Billy-boy."

"You don't know—"

"I know you better than you think. Now." The coaxing became a command. "Take your scalded manhood and get out. And, Billy..." In her shadowy limbo Beth heard a low, beautiful chuckle. "I think you should leave this lady alone. Next time, you might not be so lucky. She's more woman than you can handle."

"Damn you, Slade!" The curse rose shrilly then faded to a groan of pain cut short by the slam of a door.

Silence, blissful peace. Footsteps approached. Then hands were touching her, big hands, moving from her head to the hollow at her throat. Curiously gentle, they stroked her cheek, then trailed over her body, touching neck and shoulder, brushing over breasts, probing the ribs beneath. She wanted to open her eyes, but they were held fast by the weight of her tears.

"Bert!" His call rumbled over her, summoning help from the kitchen. "Bert, have you gone deaf? Where are you?"

"Not here," Beth managed, delighted that her voice worked. "Daughter...a baby."

"You're here alone?" He cursed softly under his breath. "I almost didn't come tonight. It's a damn good thing I changed my mind."

Beth tried to nod, and regretted it profoundly. She winced and lay still, wishing she could see him.

The air stirred, footsteps reverberated through the tile floor. Until it faded, she hadn't realized that a subtle fragrance drifted about her like a pleasant memory. As the cloying staleness of the diner intruded, she longed for its crispness. In the space of a breath, it returned, wonderfully closer.

"I found some things in the kitchen first-aid kit," he told her as he applied ointment to her scalded wrist and wrapped it with gauze. Then a warm, damp cloth swirled gently over eyelashes that were glued to her cheeks.

"I'm sorry. I didn't mean to cry."

"These aren't tears, little one." The cloth left her then returned, warmer, moister. "He cut you with his ring."

"Cut me?" She was puzzled, her recollection a jumble.

"When he hit you. It's a small cut, but more than there should be." His voice flowed over her, as comforting as his ministrations, even when it dropped to a grim growl. "He was too quick for me. By the time I realized he wasn't bluffing, he had a lap full of coffee and you were on the floor."

"Strange eyes," she muttered, remembering the light of madness flaring in a contorted face. "So pale."

She heard gentle music again in his command. "Lie still and look at me. I'd like to see the color of *your* eyes."

Carefully, she obeyed. He was so close, his features were a blur. All she could see was her own reflection in the black glitter of his gaze. There was a stillness in his look, reaching beyond color and light, searching. Searching? For what?

She would have smiled then, if the effort hadn't been too great. A cut and a few bruises surely weren't enough to send her into flights of fancy. But was the throbbing intensity that flowed like a current between them only fancy? Beth winced at her thoughts and stifled a groan. He was only checking for constricted or uneven pupils.

"I don't have a concussion." Her words tumbled out in a husky rush. "Archer just knocked the wind out of my sails."

"They're blue and beautiful," he said, as if his only concern were truly the color of her eyes. When his gaze slid away, he added, "You probably don't have a concussion, and I don't think your ribs are broken, but just to be safe, we should get them checked. There are no doctors in Sunshine, but there are three a few miles down the road in Laurenceville.''

"My ribs aren't broken this time."

"This time?" His eyes widened fractionally in surprise. "What would a beautiful woman know about broken ribs?"

"Enough."

"Are you a doctor, then, hiding incognito in Sunshine?"

"I'm not hiding," Beth blurted out. She struggled to a sitting position before she realized that he had accepted her terse answer and turned to a lighter note. He was teasing her! "I'm only a waitress who's more than grateful for your help, Mr. Slade."

"Just Hunter, Hunter Slade."

"Thank you, Hunter Slade," she said gravely, determined to ignore his sudden look of doubt. She hadn't told a complete lie. She was a waitress. "I'm glad you were here," she added. "I underestimated Archer."

"You know his name?"

"Not before you used it," she answered. Then, feeling foolish sitting on the floor conversing with a stranger kneeling over her, she tried to rise.

"Easy does it." His arm was at her back, lifting her from the floor. Then his hands were curling about her arms, warm and strong as he steadied her. She tried to step away from him and swayed unexpectedly. A beautiful laugh surrounded her as his hold tightened a little. "Don't be in such a hurry. You'll be a little rocky for a minute, but it'll pass. By tomorrow, if we're both right, except for a blistered wrist, a bruised rib and a hell of a shiner, you'll be good as new."

"You speak from experience?" Her gaze swept his towering height. He was even bigger and more powerful than she thought.

Hunter Slade looked down at the woman. For the first time, he truly looked. Before, he'd had to content himself with covert glances. Through a curtain of downcast eyelashes, he'd watched her move among the tables: strong, elegant thighs gliding beneath the clinging uniform; slender hips swaying in unconscious rhythm; breasts too full for her willowy leanness; the mane of tawny hair tumbling about her shoulders like a waterfall. Her smile, quick and as bright as the sun, hiding a shadow of sadness.

He didn't know her name, where she came from or where she was going. He didn't care. There was simply pleasure in watching her. And sometimes, he wondered about her sadness.

"Did I say something wrong?"

"No," he answered quickly. "Why would you think that?"

"You were so quiet." She paused, the memory of her own secret troubles crowding in. "I didn't mean to pry."

"You weren't. My checkered past is common knowledge. If you haven't heard it, some well-meaning citizen will make certain you do. You'll understand then that I do speak from experience." Something black and bitter flickered in his expression. "I've survived a barroom brawl or two."

Beth fought the shocking urge to touch him, to offer comfort for his nameless hurt. She dared not. He was a stranger; she knew nothing about him. He had come to her aid and she was grateful, but what could she offer in return? Friendship, concern? Integrity? In time, he would scoff and brush them aside as worthless, just as Eric had.

"It's past closing time," Hunter said a little brusquely, as if his revelation unsettled him. "Is there anything I can help you with?"

She risked the barest shake of her head. "The little I have to do will take only a few minutes."

"I'll wait."

"There's no need. I'm sure I needn't be concerned about Archer anymore."

Hunter chuckled then sobered. "He isn't hurt half as badly as he thinks, but now that the adrenaline has stopped, he'll remember every drop of that coffee. In the past, when he was defeated, he ran. This time, maybe he'll hobble back to whatever city and whatever sewer he left."

Beth smiled and extended her hand. "I don't know what I would have done without you, Mr. Slade."

"Hunter," he corrected, his hand enveloping hers. His gaze drifted over her, not missing the sudden rise and fall of her breasts or the quivering breath caught and held as he stroked her palm. His marauding eyes softened, lingering at her flushed cheeks. She was tempting, a woman meant for more than admiration, a woman meant to be held and caressed and loved. Beyond her quiet serenity burned the heat of passion. He recognized it beneath her icy control, in her anger. But no matter how strong or how consuming they might be, they were the passions of a lady, and regrettably, ladies were beyond his experience. He was too rough, too primitive. Even for a lady down on her luck, trapped in a two-bit diner in a nowhere town.

"Hunter," she said softly. "A strong name for a strong man."

At the sound of her cultured tone, he knew he'd been right. This brave little waitress would be more at home dressed in silk and lace, with the glow of pearls about her neck. Her natural setting was a drawing room, not a diner stinking of grease and unwashed bodies. She was meant to be cared for and protected, not left to fend off the advances of men like Billy Archer.

Hunter looked down at the hand that curled in his. They were light and dark. Ivory and copper. Fire and ice. He felt the ache of desire. She was all the things he'd never had. All he wanted. His lip curled in disgust. Was he any better than Archer after all? It was not a pleasing comparison. He had enough to reproach himself for without adding more. A sudden surge of irrational anger blamed her for making him feel things he shouldn't and want things he could never have.

He dropped her hand and spun away. With an angry gesture, he stalked to the door, ripped it open then stood staring out at the bank of white sealing them away from the world. He drew one long rasping breath, filling his chest with it, holding it, slowly releasing it, controlling himself. His shoulders relaxed, the grip of his fingers eased. Even as he reminded himself he must not get involved, for her sake as well as his own, he was turning to her.

Hunter saw the shock on her face. She couldn't know what had gone on inside his head or the reasons for his abrupt withdrawal. She had no idea who he was, what he was, what he'd done. Not yet. Now that the unexpected threat of Archer was diffused, he could step completely out of her life as he'd intended. Perhaps she would remember him kindly, as a stranger who was there when she needed him.

It was past time for him to go. "Are you sure you're all right?" he asked.

"I'm fine." Her assurance dropped into a well of silence. The emotion that contorted his face like a mask slid quietly away, yet he was left on the edge of tension.

Beth had lived with tension long enough to recognize it. His body was taut, his jaw clenched, a muscle pulled at his cheek. At his temple, a pulsing throb matched the beat of her own heart. She understood none of this. Not his sudden burst of bitterness, the anger, the indecision or, most of all, her own response. She was bewildered and surprised. No man had ever affected her as he had. But with his savage look and the voice of an angel, Hunter Slade was no ordinary man. He was an enigma. He was unpredictable. Whispers from her past cautioned that unpredictable men meant disaster.

Hunter started to speak, to move toward her. Then, with that long, slow, half-held breath she'd seen before, he shook his head. "Goodbye, little one." He said it firmly in that bewitching voice, as if he were telling himself as well as her. Then the door was closing behind him and he was gone.

Beth stared into the thick glass panel, her image mirrored by the darkness beyond. The bruised, wounded face that floated there was as unfamiliar as her thoughts. Hunter Slade was more than she could comprehend. He had sat silently sipping coffee, hardly acknowledging her existence; had come to her rescue, baiting her tormentor with a mocking ruthlessness, stripping away the last shred of pride; had bathed her face with a gentleness she would've thought impossible for a man of his size. He'd been considerate, even friendly, then without warning, he'd stalked away in anger. Yet when he turned, his gaze touching every part of her as if committing her to memory, there had been sadness in his goodbye.

Goodbye. The word echoed through her mind. A whisper like the wind through a lonesome valley, a cry for dreams not yet dreamed. Goodbye, not good-night. Hunter would not be coming back.

A coldness seized her, defying the heat of the room. The weight of fatigue bore down. Her arms cramped from lifting heavy trays, pain twisted down her legs and pooled in her feet. Her wrist burned, her face hurt. The tiny cut ached like a rip from cheek to chin. More than anywhere, she hurt inside for the empty life she'd lived and the uncertainty ahead. How could she live a life peopled with men like Archer, who leered at her and mauled her, making obscene demands? Or like Hunter, who turned away in mysterious anger.

Or like Eric, who considered her a beautiful ornament, never his wife. Who tormented her and hated her, wanting only to possess her. Who would not let her go.

Nausea churned, its heat burning away the cold. Sweat beaded her face, and the stink of her own blood filled her nostrils. Her body convulsed. She broke into a desperate, staggering run to the ladies' room.

Some time passed before Beth stepped from the diner into the fog. The breeze that brought the cool swirled about her, leaving behind its kiss of moisture. She breathed in the air, cleansing the staleness of the diner from her lungs. Her sickness had passed. As she began the long walk to her rooming house, she was determined to put the evening behind her.

At first, she moved surely over the deserted street. Then gradually, her step slowed, her confidence crumbled. Her mood changed to a sense of foreboding. There was no traffic. Sunshine was quiet at this hour. Each night, she'd walked the nearly deserted road isolated but secure. Tonight's encounter tainted that security and she was alone in a blinding sea of white. For the first time since coming to Sunshine, the night was frightening.

Hunter sped along the curving road that led from Sunshine to Laurenceville. He was a seasoned mountain driver, but tonight, he drove distractedly and far too fast. The fog was beginning to lift in spots and, in others, was denser than before. More than once, he'd nearly lost the road; even the low beams of his lights were useless when the fog was thickest. As the Range Rover jolted over a pothole and skimmed a sign, he cursed in the language of his English father. There was no profanity in his mother's tongue.

His mind was not on the road or the danger. A vague half-formed thought tormented him like a phantom pain. Just when he thought he had it, the mists closed over his mind as stubbornly as the veil beyond the windshield. His grip on the steering wheel tightened; his foot grew heavier on the accelerator. The car hurtling through the fog was an expression of impotent anger.

"What have I missed?" His mind raced through the evening. The diner. Archer. Bert's grandchild. The woman.

From out of the darkness a shadow leaped, and then another, and another. Hunter's foot hit the brakes. The Range Rover skewed left, then right as he steered into the skid. The rail of a small bridge rushed to meet him, then drifted right as the car screeched to a halt. The rearview mirror cracked his forehead, the gearshift dug into his ribs. He slumped over the wheel.

The click of a hoof on pavement drew him from his stupor. He looked up. A deer, a buck, moved from the road into the field beyond. In his wake trailed a doe with a half-grown fawn dancing at her heels. For a moment, the mists swirled and thickened about the little one, cutting it off from the others. Caught in the glare of his headlights, its big brown eyes were liquid with fear. The graceful body trembled at finding itself alone.

She was alone. His had been the last automobile in the diner's parking lot. When he left, there had been none. Still shaken by her ordeal, she was alone and on foot in a fog that could disorient even those not unfamiliar with the land.

In his determination not to become involved, not to feel what she made him feel, not to want the things she made him want, he'd been criminally negligent. He was so eager to get away, he'd left her to cope with a world of hidden danger. "Dear God!" Hunter groaned. "She could be lost."

He straightened and reached for the ignition. The engine fired; gears ground, the transmission strained. Tires spun and the Range Rover rocked, gained traction and leapt ahead. With a tight, looping turn, Hunter was doing what he'd promised he would not. He was speeding back to Sunshine. To her.

Beth walked blindly, aware of every move, every shifting current of air. Her ears became her eyes, translating familiar sounds into distorted images in her mind. The rustle of the trees became the quivering protest of intrusion. The secret sounds of night creatures were the pad of stalking steps. Worst was the absence of sound descending without warning. Its void left her vulnerable, with the sweat of fear mingling with the mist that beaded her hair and clothing with its clammy weight. She stumbled on, body rigid, heartbeat a painful jolt. Her eyes strained to follow the dirt track of the road. If she lost it, she would lose herself.

Her legs had begun to tremble, her mind to shriek when in the distance, a white light battered at the fog. Closer and closer it came toward her, reflecting off the impenetrable mass, turning the world to a glowing blank. The growl of a heavy engine surrounded her, a burst of air plastered the clinging nylon of her uniform to her breasts. Then it was past her and she was left in darkness.

Brakes squalled, tires protested, an engine snarled like a banshee. The light flickered suddenly against her back, but there was no ground to catch her shadow. Fear drained abruptly away. Beth felt curiously light and unfettered, as if the troubled woman who stepped from the diner into the fog had ceased to be. As if the Eric Westons and Billy Archers of the world were of no more substance than the mist.

Calmly, she stood in the aura of light and waited.

Like a crouching, purring cat, the car stopped beside her.
The door was thrown open. A voice curled through the mist.
"Get in."

It was Hunter. In some way she did not understand, she
had known it would be.

Two
―――

Hunter drove carefully, conscious of the woman beside him. She hadn't spoken. Not when he'd thrown open the car door, commanding rather than inviting her into the vehicle, nor as they sped over the half-hidden road. She was quiet, lost in herself. He cursed long-broken dash lights, wishing he could see her face. Into the darkness he said, "You should've told me."

"Told you!" Her startled whisper was filled with the fear that he'd seen inside her to the sordidness of her past.

"That you had no car. I was halfway home when I realized. No one should be afoot in this."

The fog! He had been worried for her. Beth relaxed, feeling foolish at her exaggerated reaction. Hunter knew nothing of her, of Eric. For a moment, she wished her life was just beginning, that Hunter needn't know of the trouble that followed her. Why couldn't Eric let her go? Their marriage was done. Why must he haunt her, keeping her on the ragged edge, suspecting hidden allusions where there were none? "I've been nothing but trouble for you," she said softly after a time. "I'm sorry."

"Don't be." Hunter's deep voice filled the small space between them. "I shouldn't have left you. These mountains can be treacherous when the cloud cover is this thick."

Beth's gaze returned to the road ahead. The lights of the Range Rover ricocheted as if they struck an illusion of stone. "Nothing seems real. It's like walking through a dream."

"After tonight, I'd think Sunshine is a nightmare."

"There are men like Billy Archer everywhere."

Hunter's gaze probed the darkness. The sadness he'd seen before was in her voice now. He suspected Billy Archer was the least of her worries. She was running, seeking anonymity in the isolation of Sunshine. What had reduced one so lovely to such desperate straits?

What man? Like a thunderbolt, rage ripped through him. The thought of some faceless man touching her, hurting her left him shaking in jealous anger.

Hunter's hands jerked on the steering wheel. The Range Rover skidded right, then too far left. Instinctively, he righted the vehicle. A glance at his passenger revealed only a slight tensing in her dark-mantled body. She was a cool one, riding out the skid in silence. Would she be as composed if she knew the direction of his thoughts? "Sorry. My mind wandered."

She nodded. He sensed the move, seeing in his mind the sway of tawny, streaked hair across her shoulders and eyes as blue as the morning sky crinkling at their corners. With her lips barely tilted in a smile, she would be more than lovely, and he wondered again what fool could hurt her.

He was being drawn in, forgetting the lessons taught so well by the woman before her. He remembered now. He was what he was—a breed who had learned to mind his own business—and he couldn't change it. Wouldn't. Not even for this woman. The man in her life, the one who'd put the sadness in her smile, was her problem, not his. He'd intervened with Billy Archer as he would've for anyone, and no decent mountain man would leave her stranded in the dangerous mist. He was going to deliver her to her door. Tomorrow, he would speak to Bert and the sheriff about Archer. Then Sir Galahad could gallop away to his mountain lair and tend his own life.

"Turn here," she directed as they approached an intersection. "To the left, fifth house on the right."

"Damn!" The expletive was a rough groan. "Minnie Jenkins's place. You won't be very comfortable here after tonight."

"Why should the incident at the diner affect my home?"

There was a wistful pause before the word *home*. It was a hurtful sound he didn't want to hear. He'd come back out of common decency, not to become involved. At the moment, he must explain the convoluted relationships of Sunshine, to prepare her. "Minnie Jenkins is Billy Archer's aunt. She raised his mother and has no children of her own. She dotes on him like a grandmother. Her naive worship helped make him a cowardly excuse for a human. This puts you in a difficult situation, and it's my fault."

Beth waited until he pulled the Range Rover to the curb and cut the engine before she disagreed. "None of this is your fault. Tonight wasn't the first time he'd come to the diner. He was in earlier in the day, watching me. What happened was inevitable."

"It was more than that. You're lovely and he would've made a pass, but it went as far as it did because of me."

"I don't understand." The mists had begun to lift before a rising wind. A weak moon cast its pale beams over them. Though Hunter was only a blurred silhouette of gray, she knew the thick black hair that nearly brushed the top of the car was shaggy and in need of a trim. His eyebrows were heavy over eyes that were ebony, not brown. His features, an intriguing blend of two heritages, were more striking than handsome.

She'd learned from watching him covertly at the diner that his mouth could be a cruel slash across his face, but when he laughed that rare laugh, there was a youthfulness about it. He called her "little one," and at five feet seven, she was hardly that. Except in comparison to Hunter. He was massive and rough, with a hint of savagery. And there was gentleness in him.

"Listen to me, honey." He turned, taking her hand in his.

Once, she would have pulled away, cheapened by the endearment on a stranger's lips, but not when Hunter said it. She abandoned the thought, not ready for the direction it was taking her. Curling her hand into his, she listened.

"Most men are contented with the things they can't change. Short or tall, big or small, it doesn't matter. Some, like Archer, feel they have something to prove. Archer wouldn't have carried things as far as he did tonight if I hadn't been there. He might've been arrogant and surly, but when you refused, he would've shrugged it off as your loss."

"A dreadful loss," Beth muttered.

"I witnessed his rejection. Wounded pride drove him to retaliate. He had something to prove to me."

"That he was a bigger man than you."

"And tougher, stronger, smarter."

"Harassing me proved exactly the opposite."

"He's a little man and he hates it. He doesn't understand that size isn't what makes a man big. His pride goaded him beyond the limit, and you were caught in the middle of something worse than a drunken obscenity. I didn't think I'd need to interfere, and he didn't think I would." The short bark of laughter that rumbled in Hunter's throat was from disgust, not humor. "Each of us misjudged the other.

"To save face, his version of the episode will bear little resemblance to the truth. Certainly, he won't tell exactly how the coffee ended up in his lap. Your reputation will suffer in the telling. Minnie will extract her pound of flesh if she has any inkling you dared reject her darling Billy. Make no mistake about it, she's judgmental and vindictive."

"Catty remarks, whispers behind her hand, pursed lips, knowing nods?"

"Exactly."

"I've dealt with them before and none have harmed me. That won't change with Minnie Jenkins."

"Just the same, you should consider moving."

"No!" Beth said the word more vehemently than she intended. The rent here was the cheapest in town. Her salary and tips hardly met her needs. A more costly room would leave nothing for the emergency fund she needed as insurance against the day when she must run again. "No," she repeated quietly. "I can't move."

"You can't stay."

"Archer's a coward. We both know the type. He won't risk being bested again. I'm safer from him now than I was before. He was drunk tonight. Alcoholic courage. It isn't the first time I've faced it." She silenced Hunter's protest with an upraised hand. "I'm not an innocent. I've dealt with philanderers before, and I'm no stranger to vicious, mean-spirited females."

"Why subject yourself to it?"

"I don't melt in the rain. I don't cry at weddings and I won't fall into vapors at a little criticism."

"It'll be worse because I was involved."

Beth understood. She should have from the first. "There's been trouble between you before."

"Nothing more than snide remarks, a little swaggering bravado. Overcompensation for the differences in our size and his hatred for the color of my skin." Hunter's gaze held hers, waiting to be judged as he added quietly, "Because my mother is Cherokee."

"I know." Her tone made it clear it was no more important than if his mother was Dutch or Irish or Eskimo.

"Of course," Hunter said thoughtfully, "Archer saw to that."

Beth nodded wearily. Smoldering resentment had burst into trouble and she was the catalyst. Trouble still followed her.

Hunter was amazed at how easily she accepted him. Would she when the ugliness began? Releasing her hand he brushed her hair away from her shadowed cheek with long, blunt fingers. "This will heal, but he can do worse with gossip and innuendo."

"It doesn't matter."

Wandering fingers trailed over her jaw, tracing the moist surface of her parted lips. On Hunter's touch was borne the familiar fragrance that lingered like a caress as his hand moved away. "You must be tired," he said in a strange, low voice. "You should go in."

She nodded and opened the door. She was slipping from the seat when his fingers closed in a circle about her uninjured wrist. She stopped, puzzled by the sense of urgency she felt in the quickness of his action.

"Wait." As the word was dragged from him, Hunter heard the rawness of a battle fought and lost. He'd said he didn't know who she was, where she came from, or where she was going. He'd convinced himself that he didn't care, that he would not involve himself further. He knew it now for a lie. He cared. In time, he would discover, as he had before, how much the caring would cost him. "Your name." His voice was strained. "I don't know your name."

"Elizabeth Wes—" She stopped short. Her heart was a cold stone in her chest. Revulsion swept over her. She had nearly called herself Elizabeth Weston, but that sleek, so-phisticated creature hadn't existed for a long while. "Beth," she corrected, hoping Hunter would think nothing of the change. "Beth Warren."

"Beth." Hunter said her name clearly. The sound seemed to cleanse her, and the flutter of his fingers holding her wrist warmed the coldness in her. "It suits you," he murmured. "An elegant name for an elegant lady."

Lights flickered on at the entrance of the rooming house. He released her and drew away. "Someone's curious. You should go in now. Minnie Jenkins would have a tantrum if she knew I was sullying her curb." He chuckled, amused by the thought.

"Sullying her curb. That's ridiculous."

"Minnie wouldn't agree. So, good night, Beth." He was firm, implacable, permitting no argument.

Beth stood on the pavement. He was barely visible, but she knew his black eyes watched and waited. "Good night, Hunter."

She wanted to watch him drive away, keeping him in sight as long as the lifting fog would allow. By his manner, she knew Hunter would have none of it. He would not leave her standing in the darkness, alone. With a wry smile she turned and began the short journey that would take her away from him. He waited patiently, as she knew he would, as she moved slowly up the walk and while she paused beneath the pale oval of the porch light. The door had shut safely be-hind her before the heavy rumble of the Range Rover's en-gine shattered the night.

* * *

Breakfast the next morning was like breakfast every morning in the rooming house. When Beth came into the dining room, all places except her own were filled. As she slipped into her seat, she was greeted by a nod or a word or two. She sat, toying with her food, listening to the clink of glassware and hurried conversation. Offering half truths about her bruised eye, she was profoundly grateful that her old skill with makeup had minimized the injury. When the table began to empty, she put down the toast she'd only nibbled on and rose to leave.

"Miss Warren." Minnie Jenkins bustled in from the kitchen. Beth expected to hear the usual scolding about eating too little and starting the day poorly. But for once, there was a change in the saccharine twitter. The woman's mouth pursed into a tight circle, a frown sent lines running down her face like icicles, the girlish lilt she affected vanished. "I'd like to speak with you."

"Of course," Beth agreed, recognizing the request as a demand. It had begun already, exactly as Hunter predicted.

Once seated in what she referred to as the "drawing room," Minnie Jenkins took Beth's hand in hers. "Now, my dear—" the wrinkled, beringed hand patted a smooth ringless one "—I know you're new here and there's no way you could know. If anyone had even suspected what might happen, you would've been warned."

"Suspected? Warned? About what, Mrs. Jenkins?" Beth didn't mean to be curt, but she felt she would scream if the woman didn't release her hand.

"Why about that rascal who brought you home last night. And how he threw hot coffee on poor Billy. What else?"

What else, indeed? Had Hunter been right in all his predictions? Did the woman judge the world from a warped point of view, using her nephew as her standard of perfection? It would be useless to try to tell the woman the truth. Beth shuddered and tried to withdraw her hand, but the dry, papery grasp only tightened.

"He's evil, a devil straight from the fires of hell. He's been trouble from the moment he came to the valley. What you would expect from the spawn of a squaw."

Beth felt sick. It was like hearing Billy Archer's taunts all over again.

"Surely you could tell he isn't a real American. His father was English, and his mother a savage."

"By savage you mean a *native* American."

"A Cherokee." Minnie missed the sarcasm in Beth's remark. Her mouth was like a wrinkled prune, spitting her personal brand of hate and prejudice. "Such black eyes. And their hair! I've never seen so much ugly black hair in my life."

"Hunter's eyes are beautiful. So is his hair."

The woman was too poisoned by her own venom to hear. Her spitting rasp became a hiss. "Her name is Bell. *She* brought him to Laurenceville over thirty years ago instead of the reservation, where they both belong."

Beth had learned a little of the attitudes and geography of the area and knew these mountains were once the home of the Cherokee. Now their reservation was a few hours' drive away. "Why did Bell Slade come here? She must have had a good reason."

"After her English husband died, his family didn't want them. They were an embarrassment. Can you imagine someone like Hunter Slade inheriting the family title? How could a savage ever be an English earl?"

"I can imagine," Beth said, remembering the innate dignity of the dark man who had been kind to her. At Minnie's haughty gasp, she redirected the woman's attention with a reminder. "You never said why Bell Slade came to Sunshine."

"Not here, thank heaven. To Laurenceville, which is too close for me. Nathan Sinclair was a friend of her husband. He was a busy doctor and a widower raising his orphaned grandson. Out of friendship, he offered the woman a job as his housekeeper. Lord! She was in his house all the time. All day and most of the night. If that wasn't shameful enough, they put that son of hers in the same school as the other children of Laurenceville and Sunshine."

"Mrs. Jenkins," Beth asked far more calmly then she felt, "what harm could a child do?"

"Harm? He did nothing but harm. He refused to learn, fought with the boys. And later, there were the girls." Pale eyebrows lifted knowingly. "Not one was safe from Hunter Slade."

Beth heard the hatred in the name. Poor Hunter. Old, regional prejudices had been heaped on his head. "You're a widow, Mrs. Jenkins, you know that being alone isn't easy. Bell Slade probably did the best she could for herself and her son."

Minnie stared blindly for a moment, and Beth thought she wouldn't answer. But the woman was not done. "She brought that black-haired devil among us."

"A child, Mrs. Jenkins, and except for his coloring, I'm sure no different from the other children. All boys fight— it's natural—and what girl wouldn't find Hunter attractive?"

"Attractive!" Minnie leaned forward, a vicious gleam in her eyes. "Will you think he's so attractive when I tell you he nearly killed a man? With his bare hands, like a wild animal."

The world lurched violently as Beth finally wrenched her hand free. She could not speak, her silent objection was knotted in her throat. Sick with disgust, she rose from her chair. In her need to distance herself from the spewing ugliness of Minnie Jenkins, she bumped a table, sending a clutter of trinkets over the floor.

Minnie was so pleased with the effect of her revelations, she hardly noticed her keepsakes lying about her. With a smug smile, she relaxed, her frenzy sated. "Attempted murder at nineteen. Tried, convicted, sent to prison, but in a few months, he was back, acting like an innocent man. Prison taught him some manners, though. In the sixteen years since then, he's stayed mostly on his mountain, making his silly little statues."

"Attempted murder carries a sentence of more than a few months," Beth said hoarsely.

"A slick lawyer called it 'assault and battery with provocation.' Some nonsense about self-defense. But I know better." The woman dismissed anything but her own opinion as an aberration of a foolish society. "I take an interest in my boarders. It was my bounden duty to warn you." Duty discharged, she struggled from her seat. On swollen legs with flesh drooping in folds that almost hid her feet, she tottered to Beth. "Next time the weather's bad, I'll send my nephew, Billy, for you. There's a nice boy."

Beth shrank away, but Minnie didn't notice. Hunter had attempted murder, and the cowardly Billy would protect her? One thought as absurd as the next.

"Now, my dear," Minnie said cheerfully, "have a good day."

Beth stood in the gaudy room, deaf to the retreat of Minnie's shuffling footsteps. Beyond the lace curtain leaves rustled as they brushed against the window. A dog barked, but she heard only the voices trapped in her head. Minnie's, strident with her prejudice. And Hunter's.

"The last man who called me that didn't call anybody anything for a long time."

What had he meant as he baited Archer in that wonderful, terrible voice? Could Hunter kill? Or try to, like an animal as Minnie said? Beth touched the tender skin under her eye, remembering his gentleness as he'd washed away the blood.

"You still like to hurt smaller people..."

Had she ever heard such scorn? It was there in his tone. He hated the hurting.

"Get out..."

He could've beaten the little man easily. He chose to frighten Archer instead.

"Next time, you might not be so lucky. She's more woman..."

She! The warning he delivered was from her. Hunter painted her as the threat to protect her when he was gone.

The clock on the mantel chimed. Time to leave for the diner.

The fog was gone, burned away by the sun that bore down as she left the tree-lined street. The mile to Bert's was like an oven, but Beth was too relieved to be away from Minnie Jenkins to care. As she walked, her listless steps kicking dust about her in tiny spurts, she pondered the words that tormented her.

"The last man who called me that..."

She'd known in the quietness of her room, and in the backwash of Minnie Jenkins's bounden duty, that once she admitted her concern, Hunter's voice and Hunter's words would obsess her. They were the cadence of her step, the frown that knitted her brow, the sigh that whispered through her. None of Minnie's gossip was half so damning as Hunter's own words.

Beth's shoulders slumped. Sweat trickled between her breasts and soon, the white uniform was so wet, she feared it would become transparent. At least, she smiled humorlessly, if not modest, it would be cooler.

The hum of an engine began in the distance, gaining strength, coming closer. She knew by the sound it was a heavy vehicle, a truck or, perhaps, a Range Rover. She stiffened, holding herself in check, waiting. She had no name for what she felt as the vehicle passed in a whoosh that stirred the dust and cooled her wet body. The driver neither slowed his pace nor spared her a glance. It was not Hunter.

She was surprised at her disappointment. Neither Minnie's accusation nor Hunter's own incrimination kept her from wishing he had been behind the wheel. In that instant, she knew what she had chosen to believe.

In making the choice, she accepted one irrefutable fact. In his youth, fighting the prejudices Beth had just endured, perhaps before he understood the dangers of his size and his strength, Hunter had caused injury. But no one, not even Hunter himself, would convince her he intended to take a life.

"The last man who called me that..."

Echoes of a desperate boy. An empty threat, like the bogeyman called out to subdue an undisciplined child. Words. Only words.

The heat was less oppressive, the road less dusty as she hurried with a lighter step to Bert's.

At the diner, she found the sheriff and a worried Bert waiting for her. She added her version of Archer's escapade to Hunter's report and steadfastly refused to press charges. Once she assured her worried and skeptical employer that she would survive, she went to work.

The day, poorly begun, did not improve. When she'd volunteered to work double shifts, covering for the ailing daytime waitress, Beth hadn't expected a detour on the interstate to route traffic through Sunshine. Bert's was off the main road, but by evening, she was certain every trucker in the southeast had discovered the diner.

"Goodness, where do they put it all?" she asked as Bert passed her one more plate of food.

"They're truckers, sis. Only farmers eat more."

"And the coffee! They must ripple when they walk."

Bert cracked an egg into a sizzling pan. "Just stoking up for the night and the long hauls ahead."

"Were you a truck driver?"

"Years ago. Came through here, liked it, decided to stay. After twenty years with idiots like Billy Archer and his aunt and a few other bigots, I still like it."

"You were here at the time of Hunter Slade's trial."

"I was here," Bert said flatly. "A sorry business that."

"Was it...?" There was a yawning void in her chest where her heart stumbled, sealing her in a suffocating vacuum.

"Attempted murder? No way! He was just a big kid who got pushed too far. There were some who made life hard for him because he was half Indian. Whitey Pate was one of them. Hunter cracked Pate's skull in a fight that was fair only on Hunter's side. Took a while to prove it, what with witnesses fearful of testifying against one of their own in favor of the 'breed' as they called him. Hunter's ma works for Nathan Sinclair, the doc up in Laurenceville, has since Hunter was little more than a papoose. It was Nathan who got the best lawyer money could buy, and Nathan and his grandson, Greg, who finally wrangled the truth out of Whitey's pals. Not before Hunter served some time, I'm sorry to say."

"Minnie Jenkins said—"

"Minnie Jenkins is a fool, but to her credit, she's no worse than a few dozen others I could name you. We both have better things to do than worry over the likes of them. Now, gimme that plate. I think I'd better start over with it."

Bert was a kind, no-nonsense man. In the week she'd worked for him, Beth had come to respect him. She smiled at him, a smile so brilliant that he whistled appreciatively as an answering grin cracked the weathered lines of his face.

Hurrying through her tasks, Beth realized gradually that the night had changed. Her trays were lighter, the trucker's jokes were funnier. She forgot she was tired.

"Are you sure you won't go dancing with me?" a young trucker asked for the third time. Like all the others, he tactfully ignored her camouflaged bruises.

"Sorry," she said firmly as she filled his cup again. Lately, her customers seemed plagued by the desire to dance. Yet there was an innocence in this invitation. Easing the sting of her rejection, she said teasingly, "You're too waterlogged to dance anyway."

"If you want a woman, kid, go find your own." Hunter stood in the doorway.

Beth almost dropped the coffeepot as she whirled toward him. Even in her exhilaration she thought how terrible it would be to spill the scalding liquid over this innocent as she had Archer.

"You take your scalded little manhood and get out...."

Laughter bubbled from her in a lilting note. Its happy sound released Hunter from the utter stillness that held him. His eyes were fixed on her face, dwelling on the impish tilt of her lips. A look that asked a thousand questions was answered with a laugh and a smile.

He moved toward her, long powerful legs fitted closely by ancient denim, shoulders straining at the checkered yoke of his shirt, hair disheveled but gleaming and clean. A strange expression, a smile yet not a smile, leavened the hardness of his features. A look as puzzling glittered in the black well of eyes that never left her. Like a hunter who stalked his prey, he moved carefully, muscle and sinew flowing. Silk beneath the ripple of cloth. Slowly, he came to her, a big man whose grace lent elegance to the rugged work clothes he wore.

He stopped before her. His fingers brushed her hair from her face. Callused and rough, they lingered, curling about her cheek, touching her, branding her as his.

"Hunter," Beth whispered as she fought the need to turn her face into the cradle of his palm.

"A ride home?" The deep, low rumble was like a shout in the rush of the diner.

"Yes." She meant to add *please,* but the look of him and the sound of his voice stole the word from her.

"I'll wait outside." His gaze released her, moving deliberately to the truckers and the stray odd man. One by one, it touched them, measured, probed, then moved on. Coming full circle, it settled again on her upturned face. He drew that deep breath she had come to expect, held it, released it. His fingers twined for a moment in her hair. "Don't be long."

Heads turned, following as he made his way from the diner. For the first time in longer than she cared to remember, the icy wariness inside Beth began to thaw. Among these roving men, Hunter's reputation hadn't preceded him. Yet, with his sheer size and a few quiet words, he had drawn an invisible line about her saying, "Look, but don't touch—she's mine."

A silent claim to keep her safe.

With a weary astonishment, she wondered how long had it been since anyone had fought her battles for her? How long had it been since anyone cared? The answer eluded her.

Abruptly, a sudden concern for the clock swept through the diner. Countless cups of coffee were drained, food vanished. Hurrying without seeming to rush, the rough, respectful men drifted to the door, murmuring polite goodbyes. They were strong men who had taken the measure of a stronger man. Their respect was reflected in their treatment of the woman he had marked as his.

A little awed by what had happened, Beth prepared for closing, listening to Bert's proud description of his new granddaughter and voicing the expected response. She worked steadily and swiftly, her mind skirting thoughts of Hunter. When the last of her chores was done, she paused in the eerie quiet of the empty diner, pondering the man who waited. He cared enough to assure her safety. His method was one the men who frequented the diner would best understand.

In the space of a few minutes, with a single act of possession, he offered her security. The unaccustomed assurance spread through her like a warm glow.

Hunter Slade had given a beautiful and calculated performance.

Performance. As she said good-night to Bert and crossed the parking lot to the waiting Range Rover, she knew this was the word she must remember.

Three

"Sheriff Johnson stopped by the diner this morning. He said you reported the incident with Billy Archer. I doubt there was a threat, but I felt better having the sheriff know. Thank you."

Hunter looked from the road to Beth. "I spoke to Johnson again this evening. Billy Archer cleared out."

"A deputy called with the news about six o'clock. To reassure me and pacify Bert."

"Minnie's to inform the authorities if Archer returns. If she doesn't, the sheriff has threatened to close her down on the least technicality. Invented, if necessary."

"He seems too honorable for that."

"He is, but he's new to the job. Minnie can only judge him by herself, so she believes him. When the chips are down, the blinders come off, and the rooming house is her livelihood. She'll save herself. You have nothing to worry about on that score. But tonight might be a different matter. Maybe I shouldn't have interfered.''

"The truckers do a little playful flirting. Nothing I couldn't handle. Still, just in case…" Beth searched for the words to express the rare sense of security he'd given her. "It can't hurt for them to know about you. To think—"

"That you're Slade's woman," he finished for her.

She hadn't meant to put it so bluntly or to attribute more importance to his thoughtfulness than she should. Hurriedly, she said, "Just until the detour is over."

"Of course," Hunter muttered, wondering why he was here, why he couldn't keep his distance from her. He was trouble, and from the look of her, she'd already had her share. His foot grew heavy on the accelerator, leaving the moonlit landscape behind in a blur. There was anger in the grim set of his jaw.

Beth didn't speak. If he regretted the nuisance she'd been, anything she said might make it worse.

He turned to her, his eyes probing through the dull glow of repaired dash lights. "Does the name bother you?"

"No, it doesn't bother me."

He made an inarticulate sound that was nearly lost beneath the throb of the engine. At the turnoff to her street, his speed did not slacken. He kept his eyes on the road. "We need to talk."

"Yes." Her agreement was an expression of her trust. She had come to terms with this dark stranger on her dusty, morning walk. Bert had been her final assurance. Her concern that Hunter would regret his involvement in her life had nothing to do with her faith in Hunter the man.

With her head tipped against the side window, she watched him drive. As they began to climb, tall trees rose above them, their branches forming a canopy over the

twisting road. Beth felt as if they were shut away from the
world as they hurtled through the verdant passage.

Suddenly, they burst into a clearing that climbed to a
grassy meadow. At its crest, beneath a star-studded sky that
merged with the dark panorama below, Hunter stopped. He
sat at the wheel, shoulders hunched, head bowed. "Before
I draw you into this charade, there are things you need to
know."

"I do know, Hunter," she said softly.

His head whipped about. "What do you know?"

"Minnie told me what happened when you were nineteen."

Hunter groaned. "I suppose I knew she would. She never
misses an opportunity. But when you looked at me tonight
and smiled, I hoped I was wrong." The stars paled before
the glitter of his eyes. "You know, yet you're here in the
middle of nowhere with the half-breed, the would-be mur-
derer?"

"Don't." Her hand covered his as it curled tighter about
the steering wheel.

His laugh was a brittle sound. "I wish I could tell you the
fights never happened, but they did. Too many of them."
The light that flashed from within was extinguished even
before the shuttering fall of heavy eyelids. "Don't fool
yourself about that."

"I haven't. The story I heard was warped, but Bert set it
straight. I know you fought. Even before Bert's version, I
couldn't believe you were malicious."

"A barroom brawl is nothing if not malicious." The
scornful jeer was meant to undermine her belief.

"Stop it!" Her fingers cut into his flesh. "Just stop it!"

"I was drunk, Beth. A stupid redskin who couldn't hold
his firewater spoiling for a fight." He continued relent-

lessly in a voice that could persuade her to believe if she let herself listen.

"Are you determined to make me think the worst?" She snatched her hand away from his. "Why worry about Minnie Jenkins? You do a terrific number on yourself."

"You have to know, Beth. What I was. What I am." It was an old habit, painting the blackest picture of himself before others could. In a crazy way, it lessened the hurt.

"Yes," she agreed tonelessly. "Of course, I must." Her arms were hugged closely against her yet she was visibly trembling. Her voice faded to a whisper. "Take me home. Now, please." A tear shimmered unnoticed on her lashes as she stared woodenly ahead. "You're right. I need to know every ugly, twisted fact. Now that you've made sure of it, the obvious conclusion is that I shouldn't be here on a deserted hilltop with you.

"So, what does that say for my judgment in friends? Pretty poor, huh?" She lashed out, hurt by his need to destroy her trust. Was he recanting a commitment of any sort to her?

Brawny arms plucked her from the seat as if she were weightless. Hunter slid from the Range Rover, taking her with him. At the meadow's edge, he sat on a boulder, folding her against him, rocking her in his embrace until her anger ebbed.

"Hunter," she said, her head resting against his chest, "I didn't mean that."

"No matter, it's true."

Beth sat so still that even her breathing was shallow. Her anger had taken more out of her than she realized. Why else would Hunter's arms feel so perfect about her? The answer escaped her, but it didn't matter. Nothing mattered but the desolation she heard in him. Tears spilled down her cheeks, staining his shirt.

"I've done it again, haven't I?" Regret mingled with awe as he began to understand. Incredibly, it upset Beth to hear him maligned, especially by himself. Her silent stillness, her tears were born of compassion. "I'm not very good at accepting apologies, so bear with me." He drew a deep breath. "Beth Warren, your apology is most humbly accepted." He smiled, brushing the last tear from her cheek. "Better?"

"Much," she said, nodding. "Thank you."

Hunter laughed. "That's the first time anyone thanked me for accepting an apology. It's the first time anyone ever fought for me, even if it was against myself." Long fingers tangled in her hair, holding her with a waiting stillness. There was no laughter in his rough, low voice when he asked, "Do you always fight as fiercely as you have for me?"

"No," Beth answered honestly. "For a long time, I didn't know how to fight." What might her life have been if she had? she wondered. In her childhood, living her mother's dreams, never her own. In her marriage, decorating Eric Weston's life, enduring his cruelty, suppressing her own needs. If she had fought then, would she be in Hunter's arms now?

Hunter's fingers burrowed deeper into the mass of her hair, tilting her head until their gazes met. "And the tears, tiger lady? Were they for me?"

Her gaze never wavered. "They were for me."

He felt a flicker of disappointment, yet he knew that if her tears weren't for him, neither were they self-pity. "Tell me."

The dark probing look, the long fingers still tangling in her hair, the soft soothing voice were mesmerizing. "I'd found someone I could trust and you were driving me away. It makes no sense. We hardly know each other and trust should be earned, but it's there. You walked out of the fog and became the first real friend I ever had. Then tonight, you wanted me to hate you."

"So your tears were for me, in a way," he said, and the tenderness in his eyes was heartbreaking. "Have you never had a friend before?"

"None who cared simply because I was another human being. Never one who asked nothing in return."

"I've been fortunate in my friends," Hunter said. "I was something of an outcast in school, for a number of reasons, but those few, wonderful people made up for the rest. Then there was a time when even they couldn't help." His arms tightened about her, drawing her closer. Her cheek rested again over his heart. "I'd like to tell you about it, if you'll listen."

"Hunter, I don't need this."

"I do. If you still feel the same when I'm finished..."

"I will, but I'll listen." She heard the change in the tempo of his heart and felt his sudden tension, then his story was pouring from him.

In a low voice, never lovelier than in grief and regret, he told her of a child of two heritages, belonging to neither. A wild, tortured boy reaching for the oblivion of the bottle. He spoke of a bully and cruel taunts; of lashing out in forgotten strength; of life-threatening injuries; long, endless days of prison, mercifully ended by appeal and pardon. He spoke of coming home; of turning to the talent he'd virtually ignored; of friends who never stopped believing in him. At last he spoke of a dream; of walking a land without prejudices with his head held high.

Beth heard, wishing she could temper the hurt. Yet she could only listen.

Hunter grew silent, his story was done. He sat in total stillness, drawing comfort from her. It had been so long since he'd held a woman in his arms or felt the soft crush of breasts against his chest or the beat of a heart's pulse beneath his lips. So long since his hands had explored silken curves. Longer still since desire like this had come to him, lacerating like the secret cut of a razor, known only in its keening edge of hunger and need.

He touched a vein that ran like a blue ribbon across her temple, her life flowed beneath his fingertips. His fascination with her was a living thing, increasing, demanding. But this was not some barroom chippy who would smile and play her role, mechanically meeting the needs of lust. This was Beth, who listened in distress as he painted himself ugly in her eyes. Who made him forget the wounds inflicted by another woman. Who had never had a real friend.

His sigh was a ragged rasp as he set her from him and rose. Facing the night-shrouded land, he said softly, "I nearly killed a man in drunken anger, Beth." He lifted his hands before his face. "I've lived a violent life, and there's nothing I can do to change it." He turned, his eyes seeking hers in the cool, white light of the stars. "Is that the sort of friend you want?"

"Yes," she said simply.

"I'm an outcast. By marking you as my woman, I've branded you the same. The day might come when you hate me for it."

"You aren't going to drive me away, Hunter. If the choice is mine, then I've decided." She took the steps needed to bring her to his side and took his hand in hers. "I never knew what a real friend was. Now that I do, I won't lose you."

Hunter's fingers laced through hers as he drew her nearer. With the honesty that had driven him to tell her of his troubled youth, he said, "You know there's more than friendship between us."

She knew he wanted her. The creature she had been had learned to sense the lust in men. She saw hunger flash in his eyes and felt it burn in his body. The chained heat of it had kindled a response in her that would one day demand release. Then she would have to tell him what she had been.

Would he want her when he learned of the emptiness of her existence—that she had been groomed from birth to be the ultimate opportunist, trading beauty and self-worth for wealth and a loveless marriage? When he knew, could he look at her as he did now, with passion tethered only by brutal self-control? Would there be in her this fierce shuddering need only he awakened with his sweet, rough tenderness?

She wanted to tell him, to be as honest as he had been. She couldn't. Not yet. Just for awhile, she wanted to keep this beautiful friendship that trembled on the brink of love. Her eyes were heavy lidded, her voice shook as she answered, "I know."

"Just so you do," Hunter said. Then, deliberately, he changed the subject. They'd made a beginning. For now, it was enough. "There's something I want to show you." His arm dropped lightly about her shoulder as he guided her closer to the precipice. "There." He pointed to a constellation hovering above the invisible horizon. "Do you see the star just to the left of the two larger ones?"

"I see it." Her hair tangled in the fine, dark down scattered over his arm as she nodded. "It looks almost blue."

"Look directly beneath it at the cluster of lights." He guided her with a slight pressure on her shoulders.

"Yes! I see them."

"That's my home. The whole mountain is mine. My friends live in the village below. To them, I'm simply Hunter. Nothing else." The pressure of his fingers on her shoulder was excruciating. "Just Hunter."

"Never Hunter Slade, the Cherokee sculptor?"

"You know that, too?" He was only mildly surprised.

"I didn't at first. Billy Archer and Minnie made sense-
less comments. Taken together, they triggered a memory.
Your name, your background, the mountains, there were
too many similarities to be coincidence. You confirmed it."

"Did I?"

She realized he had little recollection of the story that had
poured from him or of the glimpses of pain he revealed. As
his fingers tightened, she struggled to keep her own pain
from her face. He must not see that he hurt her. Gradually,
the pressure eased, but too late. Tomorrow, she would bear
the murky marks of his fingers on her shoulders. She began to understand how one with such incredible strength
could misjudge it, despite the most desperate caution. Was
it any wonder he withdrew within his talent and spoke of his
home as a haven. "I'd like to see your home someday."

"I'd like that, too. Right now, I'd better get you back to
your place." He hesitated, a frown gathering on his face.
"Since you insist on staying there, you won't let Minnie
change your mind?"

"About you? Not a chance." She grinned up at him and
with her arm about his waist, strolled with him to the Range
Rover.

"See ya, Hunter." The trucker dug into the pocket of his
jeans, scavenging change for Beth's tip, and nodded to Bert,
but it was to Hunter he spoke.

Beth paused in her work as she watched. How many times
in the past three weeks had she seen this? As the drivers became regulars for the duration of the detour, they'd settled
into a routine. They ate hugely of Bert's plain fare and
watched her with open appreciation. But it was to Hunter
that they were drawn. His quiet, unassuming strength rein-

forced their own strengths. How often, she mused, had she seen a late-night traveler dawdle over his meal, waiting for Hunter to appear, to exchange a word or to share a laugh? Their respect was hard earned, but to Hunter, they gave it unquestioningly.

Hunter waited patiently for her and never noticed.

Only the occasional valley dweller noticed. One foolish soul had taken it upon himself to complain. Choosing a time when the diner was nearly deserted, he'd lectured an ominously silent Bert on the foolishness of allowing one of Hunter Slade's ilk to sully the diner. Truckers were bad enough, but Hunter Slade? Beth had turned away to hide her laughter when Bert presented the "sanctimonious bastard" with his proverbial hat and invited him not to hurry back. When he'd stumbled through the door, helped along by Bert's hand at the seat of his pants, he'd heard, as Beth had, that if this was an example of the decent citizenry of Sunshine, Bert would take the *ilk* of Hunter Slade anytime!

Now Beth began each day anticipating its end. The moment when Hunter waited in the doorway, framed by the night beyond, was the focal point of her life. He came and something inside her quickened and soared. Her smile held a special glow. She felt it, she knew he did, too. He stood each night waiting for its touch; only then did he step into the diner. They rarely exchanged more than a greeting. Words would come later when they were alone. The drive to the rooming house was filled with detours and delays. Their favorite spot was the meadow. There, they walked and laughed and talked with Hunter's arms comfortably about her. Yet both knew that passion lurked beneath the gentle veneer. They played a waiting game, and time was running short.

Bert's faith in Hunter, and Hunter, himself, gave Beth the strength to endure the growing coolness at the rooming house. Her pleasure in their time together helped her ignore the stares and whispers and the fact that someone had rifled through her meager possessions with a careless hand. It was the sort of thing Eric would do, but she would not let herself believe he had found her. When days of watchful waiting passed and Eric did not appear, she finally believed her inquisitive landlady was her intruder.

Beth ignored Mrs. Jenkins's meddling as she did the blatant insults. She had to ignore them. Bert paid her as much as he could, just more than enough to cover the rent. The lofty gesture of a grand exit was beyond her. There was nowhere she could go. Swallowing her pride, she suffered the indignities and hoped Hunter would never know.

"Hey, tiger lady, why such a frown?"

"Hmm?" Beth looked up as Hunter's teasing brought her to the present.

"Scrub any harder, the paint will come off that table. Get your purse." His voice softened. "I'm taking you home."

"Not yet. Bert needs me."

"For what?" Hunter asked as he gestured toward the empty room. "Get your purse, Beth."

She nodded obediently, too tired for argument. She barely managed a goodbye for Bert before Hunter led her away. For the first time, he kept her close to him with his arm about her as he drove. His warmth chased away her worries. In the encircling shelter he offered, she could forget. Slowly, her eyelids closed.

Hunter knew the instant she fell asleep. The spiraling coil that had drawn her tighter and tighter over the past weeks began to unravel until her body grew slack against him. Her breath was soft. Her hair spread over his shirt, touching the bare skin of his arm in a tantalizing caress. Eyelashes that lay like shadows on her cheeks hid the dark circles left from sleepless nights. They were hidden, but he never forgot they were there. He'd watched them grow darker as her eyes grew bigger in her delicate face. Something was terribly wrong, but she wouldn't confide in him. He suspected he was the cause.

"Dammit!" he cursed in frustration. He'd learned to be a patient man. With the cards he'd been dealt by fate, he'd had to. But Beth defeated him. According to the calendar, he had known her for weeks, yet their time together had been short. An hour here, a half hour there, less than twenty-four hours. In less than a day, she'd become a necessary part of his life. In these late hours when time flew, he'd allowed her into his life as he'd never allowed anyone before. She'd laughed with him, talked with him and listened to him. She knew his pain and guilt, his dreams, but what did he know of her? Only that yellow was her favorite color, for it was the color of the sun; she liked wildflowers and kittens and butterflies, and coffee with the rising sun; she hated to be told she was beautiful; and sometimes, she was far away, lost in a melancholy world of her own.

He had no idea where she came from, where she was going and what she was running from, and it didn't matter. There were always secrets. He had his own; she was entitled to hers. Now something had gone wrong in the part of her life that touched him, the part that he could change and set right if she hadn't shut him out. Day by day, he watched her grow quieter and thinner, her smile faded. He'd hoped she would confide in him, but she faced her troubles alone.

Hunter brought the Range Rover to a halt before the rooming house. Carefully, he cut the engine and doused the lights. Beth responded to his moves by snuggling closer, her lips grazing the flesh at the base of his throat, her breath cooling the heated flush of his skin as it fanned a smoldering need. He shrugged aside his physical distress. It was Beth who troubled him.

He released the pent-up sigh that lay trapped in his lungs and forced the tautness from his body. Beth slept the sleep of exhaustion. If she found refuge from her problems in his arms, he would hold her until dawn if need be. Any who saw and gossiped be damned, he thought as he settled himself for the duration.

He had no idea how long he'd been holding her when he drifted off. The probing glare of approaching lights flickered over them, splintering through his quiet sleep. "What the devil!" He threw his free arm over his face in an unthinking reaction. Then, as quickly as it had come, the car was past and night returned. For a rare unguarded moment, he was disoriented, then Beth stirred against him and he remembered.

She was as soft as a kitten. Her skin was moist like the early-morning dew. With the rise and fall of each breath, her breasts brushed against him, each gentle touch snatching his own breath from his body. Her lashes fluttered, teasing his flesh like a dancing butterfly. She murmured something that ended in a long sweet sigh but did not waken. Her hand slid over his chest beyond the open collar of his shirt, burrowing beneath the fall of his shaggy dark hair and curling about the heated flesh of his nape. Hunter bit back a groan as she drew him closer.

He held himself in check, struggling against primal instincts that urged him to slide his hands into her tousled hair and lift her face to his. His lips ached to kiss her sleep away, leading her with him beyond the comfortable security she treasured to the hungering need that lay, waiting, between them. He wanted her, his body would not allow him the luxury of a lie, but with Beth, he wanted more than the quenching of lust. He wanted to draw her to him and lose himself in her in a sweet intimacy he'd never known.

He muttered to himself, a low, unintelligible rumble of denial and frustration. Beth had troubles enough in her life. Their friendship could be a double-edged sword, as harmful for her as it was good. He must not complicate her life more than he already had.

Warily, tense with the effort of his resolve, he looked down at her, remembering that beneath that lovely fringe of lashes the skin was bruised by fatigue. Rage burned in him, at himself and at the world that had done this to her. But a part of him knew no anger burned as hotly as the desire that would make a mockery of his promise.

How had he come to this? In his thirty-five years, he had learned his lessons well. The young boy who had railed against his fate had become a man who could put the past behind him. His one serious love affair and its disastrous end were no more than a dark memory. As with each disappointment and each success, they had contributed to the making of a self-contained man. He had learned to heed his mother's wisdom. To discount the prejudices of crippled minds. To view his heritage as a source of pride. To value his few friends. But above all, he had learned to walk alone, expressing himself in his talent, needing nothing, wanting no one, keeping himself aloof from the hurtful disappointments of romantic entanglements.

Then he had stopped at Bert's Diner and discovered he was no less vulnerable than any man.

Beth stirred in sleepy confusion. "You're home, Beth," he said softly. "With me." As she subsided against him, he was amazed that despite the hours she worked in the diner, it was the fragrance of the wildflowers she loved that clung to her shimmering hair. He felt her head turning, lifting, sensed the touch of her gaze before he met it. She was drowsy, contented and defenseless. The trust he saw in her face was the most beautiful thing he'd ever known.

"Hunter," she murmured, a needless invitation as, heedless of lessons learned or promises made, his dark head descended with aching slowness to touch his lips to hers.

Her mouth was as inviting as it looked. Soft, honeyed flesh yielded to the gentle pressure of his kiss. Her hand touched his face, curving about his jaw, lingering at his temple. A faint whimper shook her, and its low delicious sound burned through him with the white-hot glory of summer lightning.

His heart pounded against her breasts. A thin barrier of clothing veiled the mystery of their bodies but not the fury of desire. She touched him, and everywhere her fingers explored, her lips followed like a sculptor, twice learning the clay—over his cheeks, his brow, his eyelids, a feather-light tracing followed by the fleeting caress of velvet. He suffered her exquisite torment, his mind and body in chaos. His determination to follow only where she led diminished with each gentle foray.

He hurt, and he had never known that pain could be so sweet. He endured, responding, reacting, never initiating. When he thought the touch of her lips had drawn him to the pinnacle of love and desire, she murmured again a low appeal. Her hand slid from his face into his hair, drawing him closer, her lips parting, seeking the wild hunger in him, releasing him from unspoken promises. With a ragged cry, Hunter stepped beyond the realm of desperate restraint into a land where he'd never gone.

The cramped quarters of the Range Rover was no hindrance. He was hardly aware of his surroundings as he embraced her, stroked her, the gentle savage within him reveling in the rising tide of her answering passion. Impatiently, he tugged at the buttons of her uniform. One by one, they slipped free, revealing the flawless line of her full breasts. The lace of her bra was delicate, the fragile hook no deterrent. He simply brushed it aside, his fingers possessing a magical sureness in his quest.

She was lovely in the reflected light of a summer moon, as if she were sculpted of candlelight and roses. He caressed her, taking in his big hands the weight of her breasts, wondering at the softness, the utter perfection. If her lips were velvet, here, indeed, was the warm glow of candlelight and the hardening nipple a beautiful rose nestled in his palm.

He would sculpt her someday. Like this, with her body responding to his. He would capture this magic. A memory, just for himself. Someday... He lost the thought as he leaned to take the tender bud in his mouth to suckle. No rose was quite so perfect, no nectar as intoxicating.

"Hunter," Beth cried breathlessly.

A wave of cold pierced his gut; his stroking fingers grew rigid. His name drew him back from the brink of madness. Before, her voice had been drowsy with the restful sleep she so desperately needed. Now it was urgent with desire, and he wanted her. Here. Now. Tumbled on the seat in the heat of lust and sex.

He could not. The coldness in him was the revulsion of self-disgust. Only minutes ago, she had looked at him with a trust that was rare and precious. She was exhausted and troubled; he offered comfort and she'd been grateful. Then he betrayed her.

"God forgive me," he groaned, his body clenched against the shudder that threatened. Then carefully, with fingers that were no longer sure, he drew the cotton lace of her bra over her breasts and gathered the lapels of her uniform together. Buttons were beyond him, yet he tried doggedly, until silently, Beth pushed his hands away and closed them herself. When she'd finished, her hands dropped loosely in her lap and she sat staring down at them. Hunter looked at the spill of shining hair that hid her face and searched for words that would make her understand. He knew no grandiose speeches, but it didn't matter. Grandeur wasn't what she needed.

She lifted her head, shook back her hair and met his gaze. He saw no rebuke. She understood.

"I'm sorry," he said unsteadily.

"Don't be. We both knew it was going to happen."

"We could have chosen a better place."

"I don't think the choice was ours, or the circumstance." She took a deep breath and looked away. "Maybe we should let this cool down a bit, not see each other for a while."

"How would you get home after work?"

"If Bert can't bring me, I can walk."

"No! I will."

"Hunter, Minnie's sitting by the window in her bedroom. She watches every night. She can't see a lot, but with her lurid imagination, she doesn't have to."

"She chooses to think the worst of you because of me."

"What she thinks of me doesn't matter. What's important is that I'm drawing you out of your privacy into public scrutiny, and how I feel about myself because of what's happened between us." She shrugged, deliberately minimizing the importance of the latter.

"I see," he said grimly.

"I don't think that you do, but someday you will."

"All right," he agreed, suddenly sick with the feeling that because of him, her life here was a living hell. "How long does this exile last?"

"A week or two." Long enough to regain some perspective, exert some emotional control. Hunter wanted to make love to her. She wanted him, but there were things he must know. Perhaps by distancing herself from him for a time, it would be easier to speak of her mother, her marriage and Eric.

"If that's how you want it, that's how it will be." Hunter opened the door and slid from the seat, drawing her with him. As he set her down, he stood looking at her, memorizing her face. A ridiculous exercise for he carried her image with him always, perfect in every detail. With his thumb, he traced her lips in the kiss he dared not give her. His eyes, blacker than a starless night, held her. After a moment, he stepped back, setting her free.

Turning away in a rush, she ran up the walk. His eyes were on her; she felt them. It took all her strength not to run back into his arms. It was not until she closed the door behind her that she believed she had really walked away from him.

Hunter waited, staring at the closed door, hoping she would come back to him, knowing she would not. After a time he, too, turned away.

Four

The sound of the Range Rover's engine was a fading drone as Beth paused on the first step. Though she knew it was far too late, she wanted to rush to the street and call after him that she hadn't meant the imposed separation, that she couldn't bear so much as a day without him. Bleakly, she thought of the desolate hours of loneliness she'd needlessly brought upon herself.

Why did she fight what there was between them? Hunter would be gentle, a kind and thoughtful lover. If by chance there was love—given, shared, cherished—it would be beautiful.

She pushed the thought aside. Impossible. She dared neither to love nor to be loved. Not so long as Eric Weston haunted her, refusing to believe one of his possessions had slipped from his grasp. Loving Hunter and losing him would be unbearable. It was best she stay free, able to move on unencumbered when she must.

A stealthy footstep sent a warning through her thoughts, its secret creep catching her attention quicker than a natural tread. Beth's eyes lifted to the head of the stairs. Nothing. Perhaps she was mistaken. She glanced at the sliver of light that shone beneath the landlady's door. Had the sound come from Minnie's room? Was she there, shrouded in her nightgown, cold creamed and pin curled, pressing herself to the door, listening? Condemning any friend of the child of a Cherokee.

Suddenly, Beth needed to get away from the sightless prying, the hushed straining, the malignant curiosity. She raced up the steps and down the hall. Flinging open the door, she stepped into her room and slammed the door behind her. With her chest heaving more from impotent anger and despair than from exertion, she leaned against the door. Catching a deep breath and then another, willing the calm to reach into the tangled skein of her battered emotions, she tried to force herself to relax. Instead, as the sucking rasp of her lungs quieted, she found herself caught in the clutch of a prickling alarm. It flowed over her like the oily sweat of fear. She'd heard nothing and saw nothing in the darkness, but a sixth sense that seared every nerve recoiled from a hovering strangeness. Here, in her bare, impoverished room, something was amiss, its order was disrupted, the air hostile.

A click shattered the stillness; light flooded the room. Like a wild animal, she stood frozen in the brilliance, poised for flight, yet too shaken to move. Slowly, as if her arms were weighted, she raised a shielding hand to her face. Because she lived every day thinking that it would be the day her ex-husband found her, it was his name she called. "Eric?"

"Is that another of your men friends? Is he at least civilized enough for the bedroom?"

"Mrs. Jenkins!" Beth resisted the hysterical urge to laugh, then relief turned to anger. "What are you doing in my room, sitting in the dark?"

The rocker by the window creaked, burdened by the woman's weight as her hand moved from the lamp at her side. Beneath the pin curls and cold cream Beth had imagined, thin eyebrows lifted haughtily. Her mouth pursed primly. "After what I saw tonight, I decided we should have a talk."

"Your 'bounden duty'? No thanks, you've already discharged that duty. I heard enough of your prejudices then."

Minnie leaned forward, her eyes hard. "Don't you act high and mighty with me! My Billy had finally come back from the city, and because of you and your pretty face and your pretty, sluttish ways, he left again."

"Mrs. Jenkins . . ." Beth tried to reason with her.

"You enticed him, played the elegant lady. Oh, I know how you did it. I've heard that high-toned accent and seen the prissy manners. I've watched you glide through my house, all perfect posture and false smiles. Anybody'd think you were a beauty queen." She snorted in contempt. "A cheap little waitress playing at being a lady! But you fooled Billy. Then, like a Jezebel, you set one man against another. Billy was no match for a savage."

"Think what you will about me, Mrs. Jenkins. But understand this, your precious Billy is no match for a real man. Haven't you already suspected it? Isn't that why you hate Hunter? Because he's twice the man your nephew is."

"How dare you!"

"That's part of it, isn't it?" Beth finally understood that the woman's unreasoning hatred was fed by jealousy as much as resentment for Hunter's origin.

"Don't you speak to me like that in my own house."

"Your house, but my room."

"Not after tonight. I've wanted you out of here since the first day I saw you with that man."

"No. It was the last thing you wanted. If I'd left, your gossip and your revenge for Billy wouldn't have been as satisfying."

In a jeering voice, Minnie asked, "Since you know so much, why did you stay?"

Beth looked away from the bitter woman. Her gaze swept over the shabby room, discovering that her possessions had been rifled a second time, as ineptly as the first. The anger she had struggled to contain erupted. Whirling back to face her intruder, she said in an ominously quiet voice, "I wonder myself. How could I be so desperate that I suffered your insults and ignored your plundering?" She gestured toward an ill-closed drawer with a scarf spilling from it. "I wonder why I never spoke to the sheriff about your petty thievery."

"My what?" The agitated woman rose to her feet, outrage setting her heavy jowls to trembling.

"You heard me. I'll be leaving in the morning, but I wonder if I shouldn't speak to the sheriff before I go." Beth opened the door and stepped into the hall. She had no idea where she would go tomorrow. For now, she was simply eager to escape the oppressive house and breathe the cleansing night air. Her parting remark was pure bluff in the hope that at least for the remainder of this night, her privacy would be respected.

"Where are you going?"

At the head of the stairs, Beth paused. "I'm only going for a walk."

"You lie! You're going for the sheriff! You had him sniffing around here one time, making threats to close me down. You're doing it again."

"No." Beth sighed. The advancing woman was an object of pity rather than scorn. "I shouldn't have said what I did. You're a meddler, Mrs. Jenkins, but I doubt you're a thief."

"I don't believe you." Stubby fingers clutched at Beth's arm. "I wish you'd never come here. First you cause trouble for Billy, and now for me. Without my rooms to let, I've got no living. I should've thrown you out long ago."

"Maybe you should have. But you needed my money as much as I needed a cheap place to live. The place is getting shabby, isn't it, Mrs. Jenkins? Rentals are scarcer, aren't they? My room was musty. It had been empty for a long, long time. After tomorrow, it will be again. Now," she said as calmly as she could, "let go of my arm, please. I mean you no harm. I'm simply going for a walk."

"At this hour? Nobody walks after midnight."

"I said let go, Mrs. Jenkins."

"No!"

"Yes!" Beth demanded. The woman was older, but she was strong and weighed at least fifty pounds more. With all her strength, Beth jerked her arm free at the same instant Minnie Jenkins released her. Without the expected resistance, Beth's momentum sent her stumbling back. Her hand clutched at thin air as her foot missed the first stair.

She felt Minnie's futile attempt to catch her as her head crashed into the railing of the stair. With her fall unchecked, she tumbled helplessly, her body battered again and again against the curving steps. As she sprawled in a bruised heap at the base of the stairs, the silent cry that clotted her throat was for Hunter.

Then a merciful darkness closed about her.

Hunter stopped as he always did in the doorway of the diner, waiting for Beth's greeting. He was not sure what he could expect. For two days, he honored her wishes. The third was impossible, and here he stood, like some gawky teenager, hoping for a glimpse of her and needing the warming radiance of her smile. There was the usual number of truckers, but the hum of their conversation was subdued. A redhead with a voluptuous body bustled through the swinging doors of the kitchen, caught sight of Hunter and stopped in her tracks.

"Hunter Slade! What brings you here?" With her hands on her hips and her breasts swaying seductively, she laughed. "I won't fool myself that it's because you were pining for the sight of me."

"Hello, Sharon." Hunter stepped closer, his smile a little drawn. "I didn't know you were working here."

Sharon sighed in mock despair. "You could at least lie and say you heard I was here and that you missed me, even after nearly nine years."

"Sorry. I never did so well at lying."

"No," the waitress said, a touch of wistful sadness creeping into her banter. "You never lied."

Hunter said nothing. He liked Sharon. He'd liked her years ago when they'd gone into a short-lived affair, a no-strings relationship with no illusions that it was anything but sexual release. For a while, it worked. Then Sharon buckled under the pressures of small-town prejudice. There was not enough between them to make it worth suffering through the sly, rude remarks, the hatefulness. Their parting was amiable, for Hunter understood very well what Sharon had faced. The ending of their pointless affair left him a little sad, perhaps lonelier, but unscathed.

His next affair was not casual, nor the parting amiable, and in the years since, he'd turned more and more to his sculpting. It became his love, his release. He had forgotten Sharon. Until tonight when he was desperate for Beth.

"Come here often?" she asked as he slid onto a bar stool.

"Fairly." He flicked a look over the diners, acknowledged a greeting, then turned back to Sharon, who watched him curiously.

"Looking for someone?"

"The other waitress." His heart sank at Sharon's frown.

"There's only me. Bert called several days ago and asked if I could help out on the night shift. I was free at the moment—" she lifted her shoulders in a gesture that called attention to her generous proportions "—so, here I am."

"Hunter," Bert called through the window between kitchen and dining room. "Minnie telephoned three days ago. Said Beth had a cold. Made it sound pretty bad."

"A cold!" Hunter was baffled. Beth hadn't been ill three days ago, just weary and troubled. "Have you seen her?"

"Nope. The only person Minnie hates worse than you is me. But if you hadn't come by tonight, I'd have checked tomorrow."

"You've heard nothing from Beth since Minnie called?" Hunter's heavy shoulders tensed as if waiting for the lash. His glittering eyes were hooded as worry built in him like a fever.

"Not a word. I called Doc Sinclair." Bert shrugged. "He hadn't seen her. Nobody at the clinic had."

"Something's wrong," Hunter muttered. Without another word, he slid from the stool and strode through the door.

Sharon stared thoughtfully at the void Hunter had left. "If he'd ever looked like that over me, and lied just a little bit, just once, maybe..." Her gaze met Bert's. Then, at the barest shake of his head, she smiled ruefully. "No." She reached for the coffeepot. "I suppose not."

Hunter pounded on the door of the rooming house with a heavy fist, then listened for some sign of response. There was none. A lamp glowed in the window by the porch, and another upstairs. Someone was awake, not that it mattered, he thought grimly. He intended to see Beth tonight. If he had to break the door down, he would. His second knock rattled its hinges.

Bolts were drawn; a white face peeked through the opening allowed by the night chain. "Who is it? What do you want?" Minnie Jenkins peered out from a white greasy mask. Realizing who stood like a hulking shadow at her door, she growled, "You! What are you doing here?"

"Let me in."

"Never!" She would have slammed the door, but his foot wedged it open.

"Let me in, Minnie," he added pleasantly, but his tone left no doubt of his intention. "I'll break down the door if I have to."

"You wouldn't dare."

Splintering wood showed that he dared much when Beth was concerned. The chain ripped from the frame; the door swung open and Hunter stepped in. "Where is she?"

"Who?"

Hunter had no time for obstructive little games. "Beth's room," he said in a dangerously soft voice. "Which is it?"

"None of your business." The woman struck a pose of haughty disdain that succeeded only in being ludicrous.

"I'm making it my business." Hunter grasped her shoulders, holding her as he might a fragile but wayward child. He saw in her crumpled expression a mulish stubbornness that at another time would've been laughable. But Hunter's patience had worn thin and laughing was the farthest thing from his mind. "All right." He released her. "I'll find her myself."

"No! You mustn't go up there." Minnie clutched at him, but he brushed her aside.

Taking the steps two at a time, he stopped at the landing, orienting himself. To his left were four doors, to the right, four more. He had no idea which one was Beth's. Eight nondescript doors. Closed doors. Nobody peered curiously into the hall, but Hunter doubted that the ruckus downstairs left anyone sleeping.

One by one, offering no apologies, he began to open doors. The fourth was Beth's. A small light burned by the bedside. She lay huddled beneath the covers, her face turned to the wall. As he stepped into the small, bare cubicle, Hunter was aware of everything: the spare possessions arranged in the Spartan, lifeless order that left no room for the necessary clutter of living; the cold aura of existing in empty perfection with no past, no future, no hope; the discordant disorder—her stained and torn uniform crumpled on the floor. The room, its lifelessness, the emptiness, was a lie. This was not Beth. Beth was warm, she was real, and she needed him.

He crossed to her, knelt by the bed and stroked the matted spill of her hair. "I'm here, tiger lady," he whispered.

Her low moan was barely audible. She stirred but did not turn her face to him.

"Look at me." He persuaded and charmed with his lovely voice, hiding the worry that clawed at him. "Smile for me."

"Hunter?" She breathed his name, the effort obviously costly. "No! Go away."

"Soon, love, soon," he crooned, "but not until I'm sure you're all right."

"Please." She flinched, wanting to withdraw and to curl into her misery. "There's nothing you can do. Just go."

"You know I can't." With his hand cradling her chin, ignoring her weak resistance, he turned her face to his. "Dear God!" The strangled cry ripped from him, harsh, guttural and awful.

Her pupils were dilated and bright with the unfocused
haze of fever and pain. Her cheek was raw; her lips swol-
en. A bruise curved like a rainbow over the delicate skin
from temple to chin. From the set of her jaw he knew her
face hurt even at his light touch. She tried to draw away
from his horrified scrutiny and her whole body convulsed.

Hunter heard a footstep behind him. Without looking up,
he asked, "What happened, Minnie?"

"How should I know? She's a grown woman. Her af-
fairs are her own."

"Dammit! Tell me what happened."

"Well—" Minnie's hands fluttered nervously "—I
wouldn't know, but I suppose it was a lover's quarrel."

"She has no lover," Hunter said flatly, and rising quickly,
he stood towering over her. "Was it your nephew? Is that
why you were so anxious to keep me from her? Were you
protecting his rotten neck?"

"Billy isn't here. She fell."

"Fell? Where?"

"Down the stairs."

"Why, Minnie?" Then roughly, "Never mind. I don't
have time for your excuses. Has Beth seen a doctor?"

"She's only bruised. She didn't need a doctor."

"Damn you, Minnie Jenkins." Hunter's voice was a low
rasp. His lips drew back, baring his teeth in a caricature of
a smile as frigid as his glacial stare. His very quietness could
instill fear.

"What're you doing?" the woman blurted out as he spun
from her and bent over Beth.

"What does it look like I'm doing?" He slid his arms beneath Beth at shoulders and thigh. "I'm taking her with me.
Easy, love, I'll try not to hurt you." The last he murmured
as he lifted Beth, covers and all, into his arms and faced the

woman who blocked his way. "Did you think I would leav
her to more of your tender mercies, Minnie?"

"You can't…" The old woman's protest faded before h
implacable glare. She pulled again at her robe, as if it wer
her shield against the forbidding man. She looked away
breaking his mesmerizing hold. Her hands twisted int
arthritic fists and Hunter could almost feel the rage and hat
that ran rampant in her. The face she raised to him was
mask of loathing.

"Then go," she ground out, moving from his path in a
exaggerated gesture. "Take her. This is no place for the like
of her."

"You're right," he agreed grimly as he stepped pa
Minnie. "She's too good for you."

"Too good? Ha!" Minnie scurried behind him, spewin
her invectives. "What's good about a half-breed animal'
leavings? She ain't so pretty now, is she?"

Hunter stopped, cradling Beth against him. His ange
raged across his rough features and turned his eyes to smo
dering pits. "I'm a man, Minnie, not an animal." From hi
great height, his words drifted over the woman, unthreat
ening yet terrible. "Beth is nobody's leavings." His voic
hardened. "And you'd better get down on your knees an
pray that the damage to her face isn't permanent."

He left the old woman standing with her mouth hal
open, her shocked breath whistling past gleaming fals
teeth. No one existed for him now but the battered woma
in his arms. Whispering soothing nonsense, he glided dow
the stairs. Beth's head rested on his shoulder. Translucen
eyelids shuttered her from him. No cry of pain crossed he
lips, yet he knew that even the rise and fall of his breathin
hurt her.

As he stepped on the last step, her courage bolstered by the distance between them, Minnie fired her parting shot. "Don't bring her back here, Hunter Slade."

"I never intended to," he said, and stepped through the shattered door.

"She's fine, Hunter." Dr. Nathan Sinclair, showing no ill humor from being roused unceremoniously from his bed, closed the door of a spare bedroom that had been pressed into service as an examining room. Tilting his head back, he studied the worried man who paced before him. Hunter had virtually grown up in this old rambling house where his mother was housekeeper. Nathan had watched him grow from a handsome child into a troubled teen, and finally, into a talented but careful man. He knew Hunter well, but he had never seen him like this. "The worst has passed. I suspect that if she had a concussion, it was mild, but just in case, I don't want her to go galloping around knocking herself on the head for a week or two."

The doctor collapsed into his favorite chair, motioned Hunter to a seat, then launched again into his explanation. "She's beginning to ramble a bit now. From what I gather, she was quarreling with Minnie when she fell—which is probably the reason Minnie didn't call me in the first place."

"A hell of a way to preserve the fiction of a sterling reputation," Hunter growled.

"It could've been tragic. Her stupor was apparently caused by tranquilizers combined with an analgesic that Minnie took it upon herself to dose her with. Fortunately, her ribs are only bruised, and the scrape on her cheek is a friction burn that won't scar. She's a real handsome woman, but for the next few days, she'll be a mite colorful as well as mighty sore. In the long run, she should be good as new.

Now—" he leaned forward in his chair "—would you like to tell me who she is and what brought her here?"

"I don't know."

"You don't know who she is? Or why she's here?"

"Neither. I now her name is Beth Warren and that she came to Sunshine a few weeks ago. She's worked for Bert down at the diner, but it's clear waiting tables isn't her calling. She had a run-in with Billy Archer. Since then, I suspect Minnie's made her life miserable." He heard Nathan's low, muttered expletive. "Three days ago, for no apparent reason, if you believe Minnie, she fell down a flight of stairs."

"But you don't believe Minnie."

"Not for a minute."

"Hunter."

"Sir?" The word held more than respect. There was Hunter's deep affection for the man who stood with him against bigotry and in times of trouble.

"If things were so bad at Minnie's, why did she stay?"

"Stubborn pride, I suspect. She seems to be down on her luck at the moment and Minnie's place is cheap."

"Into picking up stray kittens these days, are you?"

"Not exactly."

"Then she's more than a beautiful lady in need." Nathan, who saw only handsomeness in Hunter's Indian traits, looked fondly into the black gaze that regarded him levelly. "Just go carefully."

"As careful as I can," the younger man answered.

"Good." Nathan pushed back from his desk and rose. "I've given her something mild for the pain. Coupled with what Minnie gave her, it should make her sleep until tomorrow. She's ready to go, but I don't think she should go back to Minnie's."

"She's coming home with me."

Nathan Sinclair's eyebrows twitched once in his only show of surprise. Visitors were rare for Hunter, and none had ever lived in his home. "There should be no complications, but if there are..."

"I know." Hunter stood and offered his hand. "I'll call you."

Nathan accompanied them to the drive and helped tuck Beth into the Range Rover. When Hunter offered his hand a second time, Nathan ignored it in favor of flinging his arms about the tall, dark man, claiming, as he had when Hunter was a child, that bear hugs were the right of the aged.

Hunter grinned for the first time that night and hugged him back.

When the lights of the Range Rover winked out in the distance, Nathan said softly to himself, "It's time he had a woman in his life, but I wonder what mysterious trouble brought her here."

Sunlight filtered through bare windows, catching a dancing dust mote, turning it to gold. Beth looked beyond it to the forest, where two men worked felling wind-damaged trees. One was her newest acquaintance, Peabody Smith— Smitty to those he liked. The second was Hunter, his bare back glistening with sweat, his smile flashing like the summer sun.

This was Hunter's home, perched high atop a mountain, flanked by Sunshine to the east and Laurenceville to the west. He had brought her here on a moonless night. Barely lucid in the aftermath of shock and the opiate of medication, she had seen only the hulking shape of the house and the swaying shadows of trees that surrounded it. It remained a shadowy mystery as her first days passed in a daze.

Gradually, her injuries healed as she slept hour after hour in a bed big enough for a family.

In the second week, her world expanded beyond the rambling sunlit room with its pleasant mingling of two cultures. In the short forays Hunter allowed, she found the rest of his home was a reflection of her room, combining the best of two peoples, leavening the starkly modern with the richness of the past. Sculptures, some rough, some delicate, all exhibiting the passion of Hunter's talent, were a natural part of his home.

She'd grown accustomed to speaking with Smitty during his sporadic treks to the house, and she'd learned the time spent clearing the forest was a summer ritual. At an appointed time, for as long as it took, they chopped and stacked the wood for winter fuel. By Smitty's account, Hunter was skeptical when the little man first came from beyond the next ridge—one neighbor come to help another. Over the years, he'd won Hunter over, "convincing the boy he didn't keer what color his skin was. Factually, it was kinda purty." Now, Smitty was the proud owner of one of Hunter's "statues" and, wonder of wonders, it was of "ole Peabody hisself."

Beth was discovering a different Hunter. Here, where he was just Hunter, he was content. His days were spent in the forest. Each evening and into the morning hours, he worked in a studio set apart from the house. He kept a gruelling schedule and thrived on it. There was satisfaction in his smile and serenity in his eyes. The hard, grim edge had fallen away. The lovely voice became an even lovelier drawl, husky and soft. As the days of healing and discovery passed, he lavished his unlimited care on her. Sometimes he was gruff, sometimes awkward, but always gentle.

A burst of laughter drifted through her reverie, the sound flowing over her like a quicksilver caress. Unconsciously, her fingers curled about the latch of the window. She wanted to throw it open, to catch the laughter and keep it.

"I could stay here forever," she murmured. *Forever with Hunter,* her heart echoed.

"No!" The denial burst from her as she whirled from the window. Her arms were crossed over her breasts, holding tightly against the cold tremor of her body. Some things were impossible; no one knew that better than she. Yet as she'd grown stronger, her bruises paling, her mind easing, she'd found herself wishing.

"Wishing for what?" Her question hung like a plaintive lament, sadly alien in the sunlit kitchen.

"You talking to yourself, pretty gal?"

Beth looked up at Peabody Smith with his ever-present grin. Pine needles still clung to his clothing and his disreputable hat. With his bony, loose-jointed frame and his crinkled face, he was a living scarecrow. She forced a smile. "I don't suppose I can deny it since you caught me at it, can I, Smitty?"

"You could." He took off his hat and scratched the back of his neck. "But I'd rather hear what you were mooning about."

"Oh, Smitty, you'd laugh if you knew."

"Are you sure?" Faded eyes, nearly hidden by a fringe of heavy eyebrows, questioned her.

"I'm sure." To divert him she asked, "Can I get you something? Lemonade, water, a soft drink?"

"A jug of water would be nice. Choppin's thirsty work."

Beth crossed to the refrigerator, marveling at how at home she felt. Everything about this big country kitchen should be unfamiliar to her, but it hadn't been from the first. "Here you go." She pulled a pitcher from the shelf and handed him two plastic glasses. "I was going to bring this out to you later."

"It's a good thing you didn't. Hunter wouldn't like it if
you got out in the hot sun."

"I'm fine now. I have been for quite some time. I can't let
the two of you keep spoiling me."

"Why not?" the old man asked bluntly.

"Dear Smitty." Beth's laugh held a tearful edge. "I'm
going to miss you."

"I'm going home at sundown, but I'll be back tomorrow." The ice cubes in the water tinkled against the side of
the pitcher as he set it on the table. "If you're going to miss
me for longer than that, I guess that means you're leaving."

She was suddenly cold again, even though the day was
unusually warm. "Yes, it does."

"When do you plan this great exodus?"

"Tomorrow, the next day, or the next." Her nonchalance was a desperate effort. "Whenever you finish with the
wood and one of you can take me back to Sunshine."

"Well now, that's thoughtly of you," Smitty drawled.

Beth was startled by his brusque response. Never in the
time she'd known him had he been anything but kind and
infinitely patient. "Are you angry with me?"

"Hell, yes, I'm angry."

"But why?"

"You figure it out, pretty gal." Smitty clamped his sweat-
ringed hat on his head and stalked to the door.

"Smitty!" The door slammed, rattling the dishes in the
cupboard at its side. "You forgot your water..." she finished listlessly.

Moisture beaded the pitcher, flowing down its side like
tears. Absently, she caught one with the tip of a finger. Water sweet as nectar, air fresh as new snow, sunlight like
burning gold and Hunter flushed from the heat of his la-

bors—these were the things she would take with her. These and the memories of her days of peace.

Like a sleepwalker breaking from a trance, she wandered through the kitchen, stroking the old wood, touching the Cherokee crockery, cracked and stained with age yet still beautiful. Another part of Hunter.

Avoiding the window, she stepped into the hall that led past a seldom-used dining room. Next came the solarium, offering its breathtaking view of the valley. Then the library with its leather-bound books crowding shelf after shelf. She'd seen Hunter sitting there so many times, holding a book like it was a precious treasure. Yet, oddly enough, she'd never seen him turn a page.

The hall stretched before her, all dark wood and white-washed walls, a perfect backdrop for woven mats and the pen-and-ink sketches she recognized as preliminary studies for Hunter's work. She hesitated before each, wondering about the lovely model with the tumbling hair and perfect face.

An unfamiliar feeling wrenched her heart; Beth recognized it as envy. Envy for the hours the Indian model had spent with Hunter. She wondered if the exquisitely beautiful Cherokee was his reason for remaining in the valley. Was it more than his love of the land that kept him here, contending with the animosity of the people who called him an outcast?

Could anyone or anything be worth that much distress? "Yes," she whispered, and knew that whatever the price Hunter paid, his life, his talent, this land repaid it.

She trailed her hand over the graceful contours of a small, ebony sculpture. The woman from the drawings, performing a simple and ancient task of the Cherokee. Under Hunter's hand, it was an expression of pride and self-worth. The things Beth had thrown away long before she knew she wanted them.

"Nothing can change that." Her voice was soft with regret.

Her steps were leaden as she moved down the hall to her room. Blind to the warm spill of sunshine through gleaming windows, she sank into a chair. With her eyes closed against the gathering storm of tears, her body went taut with pain. She waited for Hunter.

Her wait was not long.

Five

———

She was sitting in an old rocker. Her hands rested on the heavy arms, fingers curled about the dark wood. Her feet touched the floor lightly. Her shoulders were squared and her spine erect. The gleaming mass of tawny hair had been brushed from her face by an absent gesture and fell in a tousled cloud at the nape of her neck. As she waited, haunted by a secret sadness and poised for flight, she was the loveliest creature Hunter had ever seen.

Hunter was a man of few illusions. He'd lived hard, had survived a lifetime as an outcast and, with his strength and talent, had carved a life for himself. Beyond a small circle of treasured friends, he'd known little tenderness or love. Yet from the moment he'd seen her valiantly coping in a world that had been unkind, and though he'd fought against it, he'd wanted nothing more than to protect her.

For the first time in a long while, he didn't understand himself. He hadn't understood when he discovered her in a

rare stop at Bert's, or when he'd sat night after night nearly
drowning in unwanted coffee, watching her, committing
every move and gesture to memory. He'd given up trying to
make sense of why he'd been drawn back to her time after
time. It no longer mattered. He only knew that he wanted
to sweep her into his arms and keep her.

Except, he remembered, she wasn't his to keep. Beth
needed a friend, not a half-breed lover. His body ached with
desire, his heart with sorrow as an old bitterness seethed inside him. A cold hand brushed away the curtain that
shrouded dark memories. Memories that he kept hidden, yet
were always there in the deep well of his mind. Memories of
the woman who in a strange and bitter way had shaped his
life.

He met her during one of his rare sojourns beyond the
safety of his mountains. She was a sculptress, studying, as
he was. Struggling to make her mark, as he was. When they
became lovers, he hadn't understood that she only wanted
the secret excitement of sex with a dark, brooding man with
a questionable past, or that she would not risk her career to
the real or imagined public stigma of his mixed heritage. He
hadn't understood that Hunter Slade was good enough for
her bed but not for her life. The painful lesson she taught
him was complete when she told him with the cruelty she
called honesty that no intelligent woman in her right mind
could love a backwoods half-breed who wasn't quite as
smart as he should be.

No woman ever had. None had been given the chance.

But he was older now, and wiser, and this was Beth, who
thought she must leave him. He didn't expect her to love
him; he only wanted her to stay. Looking down at her shining head, he asked, simply, "Why, Beth?"

Her gaze was fixed on some distant point. Only the convulsive jerk of her hands as she clasped them tightly in her lap betrayed the cost of her control. "Smitty told you."

"Did you think he wouldn't?"

"I never meant for you to hear it like this. Smitty and I were talking and it just burst out. Then he was angry. Very angry."

"Don't you know why?"

"No." Her fingers were talons of ice. The nails were white with the effort to keep them from shaking.

"He doesn't want you to go." Hunter knelt before her, daring to touch her. His hands framed her face, forcing her to look at him. "Neither do I."

"I can't stay." Her eyes were blank, staring, the look of the frightened fawn lost in the mist.

"You've been happy here." His thumbs trailed over her cheek, brushing the tip of a long eyelash.

"No!" Heavy eyelids fluttered down to mask the lie.

"Little liar." He named her with a rough tenderness.

"Hunter, please."

"Please what? Don't see the truth? Don't hear your laughter when Smitty teases you, or see your delight as you cuddle a kitten or pick a wildflower?" His fingers glided over her brow, smoothing away the furrows of her frown. Each fingertip left the warmth of a kiss as he stroked her cheek, her throat. "Or is it please don't ask you to stay?"

His sensuous fingers were magic. Like soothing water, they rippled over the tight muscles of her neck and throat, hypnotizing her as surely as he had with the low, melodic voice. She struggled against the pleasure that crept through her. "Please."

"Please what, honey?" Magic fingers continued their pleasant plundering, his voice seduced. "I can't know unless you tell me."

Her eyes were still closed as she fought with darkness the longing that blazed with a light of its own. Her breath came in a halting sigh. "Please, don't touch me," she managed to say at last. "I can't say what I have to when you do."

"All right, I won't until you want me to. But first, promise me you'll look at me and tell me you really want to leave." He waited for her nod. Then, watching the naked emotion on her face, he rose, commanding softly, "Open your eyes, Beth."

Obediently, her eyelashes lifted and Hunter filled her world. He'd come to her from the forest, delaying only long enough to wash away what clinging debris he could. Moisture beaded his bare skin and glittered in his hair. A shirt had been tossed in a careless hurry over one shoulder. Nothing had prepared her for the power she saw. Not when he'd taken her into his arms as if she were a small child, nor the ease with which he moved the massive trees. Not even his admission that his strength had nearly cost a life.

When Dr. Sinclair prescribed a week of rest, Hunter insisted on two. In those days of indolence, she watched from the cool shelter of the house as he attended his chores. Though she'd seen his bronzed body gleam in the sun, when he'd come to her, his shirt was buttoned and tucked into his jeans.

Today, after Smitty's angry message, Hunter hadn't bothered with propriety, and what she saw took her breath away. As he waited, unmoving except for the rhythm of his breathing, she saw muscles so clearly defined by taut, dark skin she almost believed she could see their striations. The virile leanness of the torso that carried the burden of his shoulders was startling. The mark of each rib accentuated the bands of power that flowed into the corrugated plane of his flat abdomen. His hips were narrow, and sweat-drenched denim clung to his thighs.

Stronger than she thought, leaner than she could have imagined, he was magnificently male. His English ancestry proclaimed itself in the pelt that swirled over his chest. For the first time in her life, she wanted to run her hands over a man, to feel the curls twining about her fingers and watch him respond to her caress as she would to his.

Her undeniable response to Hunter was one of many reasons she couldn't stay. She had been happier here than anywhere. She wouldn't lie to him. But what did happiness matter when the attraction between them was becoming an obsession? Hunter with his quiet strength, his incredible gentleness and his quixotic tenderness deserved a woman who could be more than an obsession.

Lifting her eyes from the clean lines of his body, she found his gaze waiting for her. Deep in the blackness of his eyes, she saw the flash of understanding. He knew what she felt and sensed her desire and her vulnerability. It would've been his ace, if he'd played it, but patient, beautiful Hunter wouldn't reach for her. Beth's throat was suddenly tight and aching. His honor and his fairness made it even harder to say what she must.

"I have been happy here." Her voice was rusty, as if she hadn't spoken for days. "It's like the end of a terrible journey."

"But?" Hunter held her gaze, refusing to let her look away.

"But I can't stay."

"Why?" he asked bluntly.

"From the first, you've been honest with me."

"Have I?" Something flickered in his face, a look too fleeting to be understood. Then a smile teased his lips. "But you, my sweet, gentle Beth, in the little you've told me, which was the lie? That you like kittens and wildflowers and coffee at dawn?"

"No." She shook her head, wishing she could look away from him. "I lied by omission." She swallowed painfully and rushed on as her courage slipped. "I'm not the woman you think I am."

"I see." A shutter came down. She could read nothing in the grim set of his face, but his voice was like a raw, ragged wound. "You're not so tolerant of people like me, after all?"

He was waiting with that quiet stillness she'd come to know, waiting for one more rejection. Despair swept through her. She wanted to tell him of the beauty and magnificence she saw in the blending of two heritages. Instead, she said, "The problem isn't you or what you are. It's me. I'm trouble, and you've had more than your share. If I stay—" With a dispirited shrug, she sighed. "I should never have come in the first place."

"I don't recall giving you a choice."

"No," she said, remembering his strength as he held her battered body. "I should have left right away."

"Still not your choice." The rawness was gone, but a strange, rough edge remained in his voice.

"Not true. We both know you wouldn't have kept me here against my will. I stayed because I had nowhere else to go."

"Now you do?"

"I... No," she admitted honestly. "But I'm well enough to look for one. I'll find a place nearer Bert's."

"Your job's been filled," he said, neatly blocking her.

"I'll get it back. Bert will..."

"Will give it back to you because he likes you," Hunter finished for her. "That puts your replacement out of a job."

Beth's heart sank. She needed that job, but perhaps her replacement did, too. "I'll find another job."

"As a waitress? Forget it. It's not exactly your calling. You weren't terrible, but you were a long way from great."

"Then I'll make do as a not-so-great waitress."

"Where? The Tea Room is run solely by two little old ladies. Your other choice is a dive. You wouldn't last an hour."

"I'll leave Sunshine. There are other places."

"How? How will you leave Sunshine when you didn't have enough money to leave that miserable boarding house?" When her eyes widened in surprise, he added, "You don't expect me to believe you endured Minnie Jenkins because you liked her cooking, do you?"

"I can't stay here, Hunter."

"Why not?"

"Please…" She stared down at her hands as they twisted in the fabric of her shirt. "Just let me go."

Hunter turned away in disgust. He'd been cruel in his effort to keep her. Running his hand through his hair, he wondered if he had lost his mind. With Beth, he had broken the cardinal rule of his life. By trial and error, he had learned the key to survival was honesty. Truth often hurts, but not nearly so much in the end as lies and self-deception. He had deceived himself declaring, as he watched her like a starving man, that he wanted to know nothing of her past or of her future.

That was his first lie. How many more were there? He turned back to her, his gaze searching her face. He wanted to know everything. The triumphs and tragedies, the joy and the pain, the things that made her Beth. "Tell me. Prove to me that you can't stay. Make me believe it and I'll let you go." He flinched at the sound of his own arrogance.

"It's a long story."

"I have all day." Hunter crossed his arms in an obdurate gesture Beth had seen before. He would not let her go gracefully.

"I don't know where to begin..." She looked down at her hands, stilled now in a frozen clasp. "Perhaps with Elizabeth Weston, who traded her so-called beauty for money. The ornament on a wealthy man's arm and his shill in the dirty world of professional gambling. The possession of the prominent but notorious Eric Weston. A woman you wouldn't like."

"Eric Weston," Hunter repeated without inflection.

Beth waited for the disgust, but his face betrayed nothing. Surely he recognized the name. Every tabloid and newspaper in the southeast had exhausted the story of the scion of a respectable family and his link with the underworld, of gambling debts and suspicious deaths. The media was quiet now, hushed up by family influence, but surely Hunter had heard. "If you knew..."

"I know who Eric Weston is and what rumor says he is."

Beth looked away, her gaze falling on sunstruck mountains. "I was his wife." The admission covered the spectrum of shame and disgrace. She looked from the window and the mountains to a bright woven mat over the mantle, anywhere but at Hunter. Her courage paled at facing his contempt. The breath she drew was a ragged, heartsick sound. "I'll pack now." She thought of her few belongings, brought from the boarding house by Peabody Smith. "It won't take me long."

"No."

Hunter's explosive command startled her. Only her wooden control kept her from cringing. "Surely you want me to go."

"Not until I've heard all your story. You started in the middle. This time, begin at the beginning. Tell me how a woman so unsuited for Eric Weston fell into his clutches."

Her control crumbled. Her brittle laugh skirted the edge of hysteria. He wanted to back away, but he couldn't. Not when it would mean losing her. Though Beth hated to tell him of her past, he knew she would not stay if she didn't. Hunter waited, silently, for her wild laughter to stop.

"I'm sorry." Beth's eyes glittered with sorrow that mocked her laughter. Absently, she massaged her temples. Then, only vaguely aware of what she did, she folded her hands tightly in her lap. "I shouldn't have laughed, but you're so wrong. I was meant for a man like Eric Weston from the day I was born. I was groomed for it. Every day was planned, every move judged." She looked again to the window, but her blind eyes saw neither sunshine nor mountain. "My mother had a dream for me. Wealth, fame, all the wonderful things she never had. She was always a dreamer. Even the drifter who promised her the world and left her alone and pregnant was a part of her dreams. She told wonderful tales of him. Of course, he was dashing and handsome and wealthy, and someday, he would be back for her." Beth smiled sadly for the broken dream. "He never came."

"She turned to you to provide her dreams."

"The perfect child must grow up to be the perfect princess and marry the perfect prince and lead the perfect life. That became her goal. I wasn't allowed to play with other children. I might damage what would one day be a very merchandisable body." She looked up at him with a slight frown. "*Merchandisable?* Is there such a word?" There was something heartbreaking about her dismissive shrug, as if she dismissed herself also. "I don't suppose it matters. It fits. In high school, I was allowed to mingle, but only a little. To ensure the right awards, the right credentials, the right superlatives for the scholarship to the right college. She scrimped and saved and worked her fingers raw so that I could have the best clothes and join the best sorority. My courses were geared to the same end. Art and music appreciation and the like. To enhance my social life, not interfere. How could a bookworm snare a wealthy husband?''

She laughed again, bitterly. ''I sound ungrateful, don't I? A life to envy, and I resent it.''

''Only a fool envies an exotic bird locked in a gilded cage.'' Hunter hurt for the child who could never play. For the young teen forbidden the excitement of being young and alive. For a good mind locked in the useless curricula of social ambition. ''Even beautiful birds can escape their cages if they try hard enough.''

''I tried. Once. Eric had proposed. He was older and fascinating, but he scared me. He was too possessive and cold. How I looked was more important than who I was or what I wanted to be. I was a decoration that other men must covet, but I was his.''

''You went to your mother to tell her you didn't want to marry Eric,'' Hunter said, anticipating her story, imagining the fear of the young girl, the martyrdom of a selfish, ambitious mother. ''What stopped you?''

''She'd learned she had cancer, with less than a year to live. She meant to keep it from me.''

''But she told you that day, and that's when you decided to marry Weston.''

''Yes.'' Beth looked directly at him. The bleakness in her face made Hunter shudder.

''Let me guess.'' His sarcasm cut like a rapier. ''After the wedding, your mother made a miraculous recovery.''

''It wasn't quite a miracle, but she discovered it wasn't as bad as she thought.''

"How long?" There was nothing beautiful in his tone.

"Five long, ugly years," she whispered. "Eric knew I wouldn't leave him as long as she lived, no matter what he did to me. Absolute power made him uglier. He intended to break me. He thought he had. The day of her funeral, I walked away from the cemetery and just kept walking. I managed to get a few of my things from a sympathetic maid. Then I found a lawyer for a quick divorce. I went into the marriage with nothing and I wanted nothing but my freedom." She sighed. "I must have been mad to think that he would let me go."

"How long have you been running?"

Beth smiled bitterly. "I think all my life. I never really wanted to be Elizabeth Weston or to ski in St. Moritz or shop in Paris. The sun is just as bright here as in the Riviera. I hated the gambling in places like Monte Carlo and how he used me to attract and distract. Perhaps it makes no sense, but the day I started running from that life was the day I stopped running from myself. I've been Beth Warren again for two years."

"It makes perfect sense. Now, what does Beth Warren want?"

"Nobody's ever asked me what I wanted. Nobody cared."

"I'm asking. I care." Hunter waged a battle in earnest now. Her wistful look nearly defeated him. Only monumental willpower prevented him from following his heart and lifting her into his arms to shield her from a world that fed on her loveliness.

"What do I want?" If her shrug was heartbreaking, her smile tore at his gut. "I want real things. Things that money can't buy. A home, a family, a useful life. Friends who don't care what I've been." Her eyelashes dropped like a sooty veil over her eyes, but not before he saw the sparkle of tears. "Friends like you."

In one stride, Hunter was before her. He knelt at her feet, not touching her, but so close, he could smell the wildflower fragrance of her hair. If she would let him, he would see to it that men like Archer and Weston would never touch her again. "Beth, would you ever go back to him?"

"I'd rather die than go back."

"Then stay here. I can keep you safe, and you can have the things you've always wanted. This can be your home. My friends will be yours. They'll like you and you'll like them. There will be some resentment and prejudice toward you in the valley because of me, but you've shown you can handle it."

"I can't just move into your home to stay."

"Why not? I spend most of my evenings and nights in the studio anyway. It's comfortable. I can stay there."

"I couldn't just live here without contributing, but what can I do? My job at Bert's is taken, and as you so graciously told me, I'm no good at waiting tables anyway."

"Stay here. Put down roots. When Weston appears, if he does, face him from within the fortress of a stable life. Security and stability can be powerful weapons."

"Security and stability?"

"It's called *home*, Beth."

She remembered the starlit meadow, the look of peace on Hunter's face when he spoke of his home and his refuge. It was tempting. Her heart twisted within her when she knew it couldn't be. "No, Hunter," she said in a tight voice. "I won't be a parasite. Not ever again."

"All right." He was thinking furiously. An unformed idea that would salvage her pride coalesced into a solid plan as he spoke. "How about a boutique or a gallery in Laurenceville?" It was a stab in the dark; he had no idea if it would appeal to her, but he meant to try. "Maybe those college courses weren't so useless after all, nor the years spent on Eric's arm. You dressed to the teeth in Paris creations, didn't you? And moved in ultrawealthy circles. Put to use what you learned then and in college. What you don't know, you can learn. You're a class act, lady. It's there in the way you move, the way you look. I see it, the truckers do, and Bert and Nathan. Others will, too. Make it work for you. If you want to give it a shot, there's a vacant building that has possibilities."

"Stop. You're going too fast. Yes, I know clothes and style. No one spends the years I did being a clotheshorse without knowing them. I don't know anything about art. Only the little I learned in college."

"I think you know more than you realize. You recognized my name, and it's not exactly a household word, I suspect there are others you're familiar with. In your travels, surely there must have been museums. Even Eric Weston couldn't take every minute of your time. So maybe you aren't a top-notch expert. A good rule of thumb when it comes to art is trust your instincts."

"Hunter, this is ridiculous."

"Is it? It's not everything you wanted, but it's a start. If it doesn't work, you can try something else."

She wavered, but hope was extinguished by memories of Eric. "Thank you for a lovely idea, but I can't do this to you. Eric will find me, and when he does, there will be trouble. I have to go."

"That's your decision then? You're going to keep on running until you're exhausted? Until the day you're so weak and worn, you'll have no choice but to go back to him?"

"I won't!"

"You'll be too tired to fight him. Stay here, Beth, and if Weston finds you, he'll never have you. I promise."

She searched his face. Hunter Slade was the best of two handsome races. "Do I dare?"

"No strings, Beth. And just until you need not worry about Weston anymore."

"You defended me in the diner. Came for me at the rooming house and brought me here. Now you offer me your home. Why, Hunter?"

"Who can say for certain?" He feigned a nonchalance he didn't feel. "It's not totally unselfish. Neither of us is a fool. We both know there's magic between us. Something special I've never felt before. Why do you think I kept coming back to Bert's for all that blasted coffee? You feel it too. Why else did you believe so unconditionally in a total stranger and fight like a tiger for him against Minnie Jenkins, against himself?" He slipped her hands free from their tight clasp, taking one in his. "Doesn't that kind of magic deserve to be given a chance, to become whatever it's meant to be?"

Her protest died on her tongue. To some, he was the elusive artist. To others, the brutal half-breed. To Beth, the man who knelt at her feet was a gentle knight in faded denim. He offered the gift of her dreams. Dignity and peace and sweet, mysterious magic. She covered their clasped hands with her free hand. "I don't want you to be hurt," she whispered. "Not anymore. Not by anyone."

The obsidian darkness of his eyes could not hide his hunger for his own lost illusions. "Some things are worth any risk."

"Yes," she said, and knew that it was true.

"Then you'll stay. This will be the end of your journey. For a while."

Her clasp tightened over his. As she promised she would, she looked into his eyes and said, "I'm not sure about the boutique, but I'll stay. I'll find something to do. Then we'll take the risks and explore this magic, and when it's time, I'll go."

"When it's time," Hunter echoed. Not before the problem of Eric Weston is resolved, he promised himself. Not before she can walk with her head high and without fear in her heart. These thoughts were for himself. Aloud, he spoke of small things Beth would treasure. "Not before the old yellow tabby has her kittens or the morning glories bloom by the waterfall."

"Morning glories? When?"

"September."

"Two months," she mused. "Then I'll go."

He released her hands and stood. When she lifted her head to smile up at him, he did not smile back. With the back of his hand, he stroked the line of her cheek. The bruises had faded, but in his mind he saw them. It wouldn't happen again, not by accident or by any man's hand. The vanished Archer, with his false bravado dwindling like a ruptured balloon, was no concern. But Weston would come. Hunter never doubted it. Every primitive instinct warned of it. No man, Eric Weston or not, would give up a woman like Beth without a fight.

Hunter's hand slid from her cheek to her hair, winding the tawny length of it about his fist. He would keep her until the inevitable was done. Then he would let her go.

"When it's time," he promised in his low, melodic voice. Then, satisfied with her promise and his own, he untangled himself from the spill of her hair and with the quiet step of his Cherokee ancestors, he left her.

Beth was nervous. She didn't look into the mirror to check her appearance for she knew how she looked. Every clean, shining hair was in place; the little makeup she wore was carefully applied. The simple dress that was several shades darker than her eyes fell demurely in an elegant body-skimming line from neckline to hem. She had deliberately understated her looks. No exotic bird in a gilded cage tonight. She wanted honesty, not tinsel glamour.

She was returning to the home of Nathan Sinclair, this time as a dinner guest, not a patient. In a matter of minutes, she would meet Bell Slade, Hunter's mother, and the friends he considered family. In addition to Nathan and Bell, Dr. Christen Steele and her husband, Dr. Zachary Steele, would be there. She had learned from Hunter that Christen, a descendant of the Laurences who founded Laurenceville, had been his friend forever. Zachary, a transplanted flatlander, was Hunter's nemesis on the tennis court. Last, and most special, there would be eight-month-old Greg Steele, Hunter's godson.

The Steele family lived with Nathan in his rambling house. Christen and Zachary worked with him in the Laurenceville Clinic. Because Hunter loved them all, Beth wanted desperately for them to think of her as more than a pretty face, more than a transient gewgaw. They must see her worth, the woman Hunter saw.

The knock she was waiting for brought her to her feet. Hunter had come for her. The dignity she had striven to create deserted her as she rushed to the door, eager for him, for the assurance his presence gave her.

The door swung wide and he filled the doorway. He was dressed as she'd never seen him. His shirt was deep turquoise, his trousers beige linen. His black hair was gleaming and neatly combed. Too neatly. This was an elegant stranger.

"Ready?" He smiled and held out his hand.

The natural gesture shattered her illusion. He was still her Hunter. It would take more than clothing to change him. Beth reached out to him. "I'm as ready as I'll ever be."

Tucking her hand in the crook of his arm, he guided her from the house to a silver Mercedes. Lifting a questioning eyebrow she turned to him. He shrugged broadly. "The trappings of civilization, stashed away in the barn for special occasions. It had a little dust on it, but Smitty helped me clean it up." His gaze slid down the length of her and back again. "Can't have the prettiest girl in the valley riding in a Range Rover."

"I wouldn't mind."

"I know, but humor me." He laughed then, his teeth flashing in his rugged face. "Pretend we're kids on our first date. You've bought a new frock that matches your eyes, and I've shined up the family sedan. I'll drive slowly through town so everyone sees us and envies me. Later, we'll drive up to Sunset Ridge and make out."

Beth burst out laughing. "Drive very, very slowly so everyone can see my handsome date."

Hunter did drive very slowly down the mountain and through Laurenceville. His gaze kept straying from the road to Beth. This was a woman who had worn silks and furs and turned every male eye as she passed. Understated elegance, classic style that went far deeper than surface beauty. He hadn't told her how enchanting she was. A poetic commentary was the last thing she wanted. Someday, he would tell her and she would know he meant more than the beauty the genes of a dreamer and a dashing drifter had given her.

At the bend of a sharp curve, he turned into a winding drive, and then they were at Nathan's. Hunter drew the keys from the ignition and turned to her, "You haven't spoken a word since we left the mountain. Frightened?"

"Petrified."

"Don't be." He stroked a strand of shimmering hair from her cheek. "You'll like them."

"But will they like me? I've been living in your house nearly three weeks. What will your mother think?"

"She'll think you're terrific. Mother understands your situation. Actually, she thinks you're rather courageous."

"Does it bother her what the valley will say?"

"When you consider who her only child is, do you think my mother concerns herself with what the valley thinks?"

"No, I suppose she wouldn't."

"The people who matter will understand. The rest be damned." He slid from his seat and went around the car to help her out. With her arm again tucked firmly through his, he walked with her over the lawn. The air was sweet with the fragrance of summer flowers. "You have a lot in common with Nathan. He loves wildflowers, too. Part of his garden is devoted to them. I'll bring you over one day soon to see them."

"I'd like that," Beth said woodenly, her cold, nervous fingers clutching the sleeve of Hunter's shirt.

He led her up the stairs and across a broad terrace. At the door, he stopped. "Hey, tiger lady, chin up." With the tip of his thumb, he lifted her chin. "You'll be all right, I promise."

When they stepped into the foyer and straight into the embrace of a stately Cherokee woman who walked to the music of a silver bell clasped about her ankle, Beth knew it was true.

Six

"**H**unter loves your child."

"Yes." Christen turned from the terrace railing to watch with Beth as her tiny son clambered over Hunter. Man and child tumbled on the library floor in total disregard of Hunter's pale linen trousers. "As much as Greg loves him."

"I've never seen Hunter so relaxed."

"He's safe with us."

Beth made no response. In the rapport that had grown steadily and surely between them during the evening, she knew Christen spoke not of physical safety but of the heart. Over dinner, as she'd watched and listened, Beth discovered why he considered himself "just Hunter" among them. Their love was unconditional. He accepted it without suspicion, treasuring it.

In Bell Slade's dark gaze, Beth saw pride in her son blaze like a bonfire. Nathan regarded him with grandfatherly affection. Zachary Steele, Beth discovered, was Hunter's counterpart. As survivors from separate worlds, they had waged similar battles and won. One was blond, a physician, born to the rigors of the Brighton waterfront. One was dark, a sculptor, highland born, maligned by misunderstanding and prejudice. Both were warriors who had worn their scars as a shield.

Beth's attention turned to Christen, who had held a special place in Hunter's life since childhood. The initial shock and irrational jealousy that accompanied recognition of the model in Hunter's most beautiful work vanished. Christen had been Hunter's favorite subject since their teens, long before he had taken his talent seriously. Though not of Indian ancestry, her classic features transcended the lines of race. In the bright moonlight that washed over the terrace, those features and her graceful body were as lovely and strong as he'd made them. Stronger and lovelier still was the love in her face when she looked at her husband.

"You're a fortunate woman," Beth murmured as she watched Zachary swing the child into his arms.

Christen smiled. Her gaze did not leave her husband or the golden-haired child nestled in his arms. "More fortunate than you know. I nearly lost this out of fear." She looked to Beth; moonlight struck fire in her eyes. "When the time comes, reach out for what you want, fight for it. Make your life what you want it to be, not what fear dictates."

"It isn't always as easy as reaching out."

"Must it be easy? Few things worth having are. Zachary's not an easy man to live with. Neither will Hunter be. But in the end, you'll find he's worth any trouble."

"Christen. I think you've misunderstood. This isn't..." Beth searched for words to explain her relationship with Hunter. "I was in trouble and Hunter was there. He's kind, he wanted to help. It's no more than that."

Christen laughed, saying, "We'll see."

"Christen." Bell spoke from the doorway, her voice like music in the still summer night. "You have a call."

Christen excused herself as she went to the nearest telephone and then out to her car. At dinner, Beth had seen that only Christen and Hunter refused the excellent wine from Nathan's cellar. Christen, because she was on duty and would take any incoming night calls; Hunter, because he never drank.

"Are you comfortable? The night is not too cool?" Bell had not joined them on the terrace earlier, claiming a few minor chores in the kitchen. Now, she moved toward Beth in a gliding step, accompanied by the nearly silent tinkling of a silver bell.

"No." Beth was flustered at finding herself alone with Hunter's mother. The older woman's dignity eroded her confidence. She wanted to speak, to be brilliant, but found herself tongue-tied.

"Hunter was right. You are beautiful," Bell said, and Beth heard Hunter's tone, his inflection in her words.

"The trouble I've brought to his life is anything but beautiful."

Bell nodded as if she were pleased with Beth's reply. "He said, as well, that you did not like to dwell on your beauty."

Beth looked into the Cherokee woman's face. She bore little resemblance to her son beyond the copper of her skin, the black eyes and hair that shimmered beneath the moon with a light that was blacker than black. "How I look is part of me, but I'm more than a face or a body."

Bell's chuckle was startling. "Courage and spirit. I should have known. My son is rarely wrong. He has the artist's gift of seeing beyond the face to the whole person. When he spoke of you, he spoke of more than beauty."

"Thank you," Beth said, the hard edge gone from her voice. She'd been given the greatest compliment. She'd begun the evening wishing to make a favorable impression, yet she was startled to realize how much she valued the good opinion of Hunter's mother.

"It isn't necessary to thank one for the truth." Bell's eyes probed as Hunter's had, beyond line and symmetry to strength and character even Beth did not yet know she possessed. The silence that bound them was not uncomfortable. Beyond the garden wall, a night bird called. A breeze teased bright, supple leaves. Towering mountains hovered like sleeping dragons. Nothing diverted the wordless inquisition.

"Yes," Bell said at last, her smile transforming her somber features from attractive to ravishing.

"Yes?" Beth queried, thinking, this, as she is now, was the woman Hunter's father loved.

"Yes, we shall be friends."

"I'd like that."

Laughter drifted from the library. The masculine chorus was led by the giggle of a child. Bell's face altered into that special look reserved for children. "Shall we join the gentlemen," she said in a tone reminiscent of Hunter. "We should intervene before the little warrior tires them completely."

The remainder of the evening went too quickly. Sipping a mellow brandy, Beth sat beside Hunter, watching, listening. Though he was an unmistakable part of the group, Hunter, too, was contented only to listen as Greg drooped, then drowsed in his lap. Beth was fascinated by the boy's golden curls tumbling in mad profusion against the turquoise of Hunter's shirt. His chubby cheeks were flushed from his play. His mouth curled in a half smile as he slept. He drew a deep, quivering breath and sank deeper into sleep.

One small, trusting hand rested on Hunter's arm as it curled gently about him.

Beth's gaze strayed from the child, all golden and tousled, to Hunter. Beneath his forbidding hawklike visage, she saw a man whose kindness defied description. There was love in the protective curve of his arm, in the tilt of his head, the brush of his lips against baby-soft curls. If I live forever, Beth thought, I will never see anything more beautiful than this.

Hunter and a child.

Feeling her gaze on him, he turned, his smile contented, wistful. Drawing her hand into his, he tucked it close to his side.

Beth's heart turned a somersault beneath her breast. His touch was velvet and steel, gentleness and power. The joining of their flesh, the twining of their fingers held the promise of a dream. A child, and a man to love her.

Her dream. Only hers. So near, yet never so far. More impossible now than ever, for the specter of Eric and the trouble he would bring was there waiting. Always waiting. Her eyes were luminous from a sudden rush of tears. Biting her lip to control its tremor, she blinked back the dampness.

"Is something wrong?" Hunter asked beneath the low-key teasing that Zach and Nathan directed toward Bell. "You look a little sad, tiger lady."

Beth looked up from their entwined hands. Hunter was watching her gravely, the jousting beyond them forgotten. His lean face was far more handsome than she'd realized, his mouth more sensitive, the glittering gaze that held hers more tender.

I love him.

The words were a song echoing sweetly through her. I have from the moment he first called me tiger lady, struggling with his apology like a shy little boy. I love him, and can only bring him trouble.

"Hey, you look like you lost your best friend," he murmured.

"You're my best friend," Beth said soberly.

"You haven't lost me."

But I will, Beth thought. If not when Eric finds me, the in September, when the morning glories bloom. She ha promised Hunter that. She would keep her promise if sh could. Her love would be the secret she took with her whe she left him.

"I overrate myself. I thought that would at least coax smile from you."

"You could never overrate yourself."

"Then where's my smile?" He waited, his eyes question ing.

Beth's answering smile was radiant, the practiced perfec tion of a beauty queen. Only Hunter saw it as the forlor caricature it was.

"I think we should get this little fellow to bed, then ca it a night for ourselves." He released her hand and move the child carefully as he spoke.

"Shouldn't we wait until Christen returns?"

"Honey, in these hills, a call can take hours. Zachar doesn't like for her to do it. Neither does Nathan, but Chr won't have it any other way. She does her share of the worl and there's nothing anyone can do to dissuade her."

"She's a very strong woman."

"There are times when Zachary calls that strength b other names. Like obstinate and willful and muleheaded."

"When she doesn't agree with him."

"Exactly." Hunter grinned. "But he knew it when h staked his claim." The grin faded. "When you care, yo

ke the virtues and the vices, the good and the bad, and
unt yourself lucky.''

"If you're really lucky..." She touched the sleeping
hild's cheek with the hand still warmed by Hunter's clasp.
er yearning for a home and a child was unmistakable.

"Yeah." Hunter rose abruptly, too moved to sit still. He
as suddenly, furiously angry with her mother, the foolish
reamer, whose selfish martyrdom brought Beth nothing
ut hurt; at Eric Weston, the cold, possessive bastard who
ave her minks and jewels and empty days of meaningless
ursuits instead of a home filled with children to cherish.
Real things. And the love she deserved. Love, as Hunter
lade would never know it.

He was tense as he moved from Beth. Greg, clutched too
ghtly to him, squirmed in sleepy protest. Hunter forced
imself to relax before the child awakened. "Mother," he
alled softly.

Bell inclined her head in acknowledgement but made no
ove to respond until Nathan finished his story. Then, ex-
using herself, she left Zachary and Nathan deep in discus-
on of the merits of a new medication. Her black gaze
icked from Hunter to Beth and back again. She sensed his
nger, as Hunter guessed she would. "I suppose you'd like
or me to take this sleeping warrior off your hands so you
an get back up the mountain."

"Beth's tired. It hasn't been that long since her accident.
don't want her to overdo it on her first outing."

"And you, my son?"

"I'm not tired."

"Only angry," Bell said beneath her breath.

"Yes."

"But not at Beth."

"No." Hunter watched as Beth wandered to the terrace
oor. Her back was straight. She swayed like a graceful reed

as she walked—the picture of tranquility, the veneer of he
beauty hiding the hurt inside. "No," he repeated, unawar
that Bell studied him closely. "Never with Beth."

"Then be patient. Whatever the trouble, it will change
Things do. Circumstances. People. Everything."

"Not everything."

"Then they don't matter."

"I wish that were true."

Bell said no more. To do so would be to embark on an ol
disagreement. She could never understand how one fatefu
encounter with a shallow, faithless woman had destroyed h
belief in love. Others could love. He knew it. He could love
He did. But no one could love him. In the heat of argu
ment, Bell asked countless times how he could be so sensi
tive to the stone he carved and the metal he cast, and s
insensitive to himself. He respected her and deferred to he
judgment, but in this, he dismissed her opinion as a moth
er's blind faith. An old argument, one that could not be re
solved. Unless, one day, he saw the truth she saw in Beth
face and believed.

Hunter leaned from his great height to kiss his mother
cheek. As she took Greg from him, he asked, "I stand mo
than a foot taller than you, yet you make me feel like
stubborn little boy."

"A mother always sees the little boy in the men their son
become."

"On that bit of Cherokee wisdom, Beth and I sha
leave."

He gathered Beth to him, and with her said good-night t
Nathan and Zachary. His anger at another mother barel
abated as he watched his own and Beth say goodbye, wit
promises from Bell that she would visit soon.

"Did I say something wrong?" Beth asked as he joined her in the Mercedes.

"What?" Beth's question jolted Hunter from his thoughts.

"As we said goodbye to your mother, you acted as if something were wrong? I wanted so much for them to like me. If I—"

"Hey, tiger lady." Hunter turned to her, taking both her hands in his. "You were perfect. They're warm, wonderful people, but they've never taken to anyone quite like you. What you saw was one of my moods. There are times my hot Cherokee blood declares war on the cool English part of me. Surely Christen or mother warned you."

"Christen said you could be difficult."

"That brat!"

"Does that go along with being muleheaded?"

"I did say that about her, didn't I?"

"You did."

"Do you think maybe that makes us even?"

"That's for you and Christen to decide."

"I have a decision for you to make."

"You do?" Beth allowed herself to be distracted because she wanted it.

"I was wondering if you'd like to continue sitting here or if you'd prefer to go home."

"Home, please," Beth said. Hunter's home did, indeed, feel like her own. Though not a new thought, it wasn't one she wanted to pursue just now. She loved him. She loved being with him in his home, among his family and friends. It was a volatile situation that could lead to irrevocable mistakes.

"Good. You need a long night's rest, for tomorrow we begin work on your shop." He kissed her fingers and released her.

The powerful engine roared through the night. Tires spun on gravel. Hunter was taking Beth home.

"Done!" Hunter stepped back, examining his handiwork. "What do you think of your door now?"

Beth clambered to her feet, putting aside the cloth she was using to dust the bottom shelf of a glass display case. She smiled in approval. The dark cherry frame of the door had been polished to a deep satin luster, and its leaded glass oval repaired and cleaned. Late-afternoon sunlight streamed through it, turning the morning glories that twined about its edge to enticing jewels for the hummingbird that hovered in their midst.

"It's wonderful," Beth said, awed by Hunter's work. "I can't believe you found something so perfect gathering dust in an old barn."

"Actually, this is Smitty's doing. He's a scavenger. When he heard you were calling the shop The Morning Glory Boutique, he remembered he'd seen this at a flea market. Luckily, it hadn't been sold."

"It was scarred and stained and broken. You made it what it is now."

"The idea of a unique door was originally yours. Proves my point about your sense of style, doesn't it?"

"It proves Smitty's resourcefulness and your skill."

"It was your idea." He refused to yield the point.

Beth sighed in defeat. No matter what she said, Hunter had an answer. When she declared she had no idea what the shop should be, he herded her down the mountain to a folk art center. There, he watched and waited as she studied the displays and learned, falling in love with what she saw. When she insisted that it was foolish to put so much time into a business destined to last for only two months, he assured her she was meeting a real need. There would be someone to follow her lead and all would not be lost. When she'd brought up the very real problem of money, refusing to take any from him, even as a loan, he'd found a solution.

The building had been vacant for years. The owner was only too glad to forfeit the first two month's rent in exchange for the repairs and improvements Hunter promised. When Beth pointed out that carpenters and painters expected a salary, Hunter informed her succinctly that he and she and his friends would do the labor. Who knew what hidden talent might be discovered along the way?

When, in desperation, she cited the expense of stocking the boutique, he had an answer ready, as well. As he had shown her at the center, the hills were filled with people with talent. The products of their talents always needed another marketplace. Beth could work on consignment, a method that was common to the mountains. Later, as she acquired working capital, she could alter the arrangement if she chose.

With every avenue of objection neatly blocked, she was swept along with the tide, and each day, like today, brought Hunter's dream for her closer to completion.

In the refracted light, the refurbished room was truly a showcase of hidden talents. Christen had proven to be quite expert with wall paper. Zachary displayed a talent for lighting, declaring that in his next life he would be an electrician, and that perhaps the pay would be better. Nathan wielded a mean paintbrush, and even little Greg tried, ending with more paint on himself than on the object of his attentions. Smitty providentially remembered a vacant house with a parquet floor that could be had for the asking. Then he displayed an astonishing skill at putting it back down. ''Always liked to work puzzles,'' was his only comment. Bell provided food and late-night snacks, and polished discarded brass and ornate mirrors that had lain for years gathering dust in Nathan's attic.

Hunter was everywhere, building shelves and display cases, painting, sanding and staining. From the initial plan to the final cleaning, he lent a hand. He spent each day with her, from morning until evening, when he returned to his studio. Then her nights were as lonely as her days were productive.

The result of those days was before her. A beautiful room waiting for the crates in the storeroom to be opened and their treasures to be displayed. "I never dreamed this could happen."

"It's all yours."

"No. It belongs to all of us. I don't know how I can thank everyone for the help they've given me." Extending her hand to Hunter, she waited until he clasped it in his. "How can I ever repay you?"

"None of us expects repayment. We've enjoyed every minute of it." He drew her to him, turning her to face the shop, wrapping his arms about her. "You did this. Everything was your decision, your choice. We were the helping hands. You were the driving force. Not one of us could have put it together as perfectly."

"I couldn't have done it without your charity."

"No!" His arms tightened about her. "I know you've never known people like these, but none of this was charity." He took her by the hand, leading her to a tall stool. Seating himself upon it, he drew her closely between his legs. With his hands on her shoulders, he said gravely, "Listen and listen well. This is lesson number one about friends. There is no charity in friendship. Don't belittle what they've given from their hearts as such."

Beth looked up at him. She started to speak and found that her voice was trapped in the knot in her throat. She drew a quavering breath and managed an unsteady smile. "I have a lot to learn about friends."

"I think you've already learned," Hunter said. "We both have." He was remembering a moonlit meadow and a beautiful woman who refused to believe he was guilty of deliberate cruelty. A woman who had fought for him against prejudice, even his own.

"Can I at least say thank-you?"

"You can. If I can say you're welcome like this." Holding her face between his hands he leaned to kiss one cheek, then the other, his lips lingering on her silken flesh. He straightened, sliding his hands from her face to her hair, holding her, looking into the blue spangled eyes, whispering her name. Mesmerized by her, needing her, he leaned again to her.

His lips touched hers lightly, teasing them, caressing, until they parted and her tongue met his. Hunter barely suppressed a groan. His hungry mouth took hers completely. Devouring her in raw, savage need. His hands slid from her hair to her shoulders and down her back, cupping her buttocks, cradling her against him, leaving no doubt that what he was feeling had nothing to do with charity or friendship.

She was like a fragile bird beneath his hands. His body moved against her. She gasped but did not move away. Instead, her hands found his face, curving about his jaw, straying to his throat, flicking loose the top button of his shirt. One by one, as each kiss flowed into the next, the buttons slipped free. Her fingers slid beneath the fabric, threading through the dark thatch that covered his chest. Then his shirt was gone and her blouse was open. Her bare breasts rose with each panting breath, brushing against him like a whisper of fire.

His hands left her hips to caress the graceful arch of her throat, following its flowing lines to the slope of her breasts.

He wanted to feel her heartbeat, possess her, hold her. When she swayed at his touch, he scooped her into his arms and settled her in his lap. With her head nestled in the crook of his arm, he stroked her breast, watching in fascination as a nipple shrank from a full-blown rose to a lovely bud. His head dipped, eager to taste it and to feel its softness against his tongue. Beth's hand in his hair drew him closer, her body moving against his in time with the rhythm of his gentle suckling.

Hunter couldn't breathe; his pulse pounded so hard the force of it drove the air from his lungs. Like blood driven by the frenzied pace of his heart, raw desire found its own expression, hotly, boldly, relentlessly. His mind had ceased to function, except to assuage the demand of his body. Beth, only Beth, binding him to her with her web of innocent sensuality, destroyed the will of a man of iron.

He lifted his head, searching the empty room. There was no place, only the cold, hard floor without even a blanket to cushion them. He wanted her. Every nerve and sinew cried its need for her, setting his dual nature against itself. The savage in him, neither Cherokee nor English, cared little for anything but the easing of his needs. The stronger voice of reason said no. He would not take her here; this was no better than the seat in the Range Rover.

Beth's beauty and body had been bartered by her mother and flaunted by Eric. She deserved better. When they made love, Hunter wanted more than barbaric lust that cared not where or when. Beth was too newly hurt, her belief in her own worth too fragile to know that whether they made love on the bare floor or in a castle, she was a woman whose worth was immeasurable.

His mother's people had a name for such a woman. Among them, she would be called Beloved Woman.

He looked down at her flushed face. She was so lovely, he flinched at the thought of hurting her. "Beth." His voice was rough, unsteady. "I didn't mean for this to happen."

"I know." She was flushed and trembling when she slipped from his lap. Yet she made no effort to distance herself from him or to cover herself.

"I have an abominable talent for choosing the wrong time and the wrong place."

"Does the time or place matter?"

"I thought it would to you."

"Perhaps it should. Perhaps all of this—" she gestured to the shop and to themselves "—is a mistake."

"No!" Hunter's hand cupped her mouth, sealing her lips. Hearing her doubt, he did not regret the denial of his own primitive need. He had used every means he knew to keep her—the security of his home, the support of good friends, the shop—but she was ever poised for flight. One wrong move and she would be gone from his life forever. The day when she left him would come. But not yet. Not until she had nothing to fear from Eric.

"This isn't a mistake." He caught her hair in an unyielding grasp, turning her face to his. "Do you believe me?"

"I'd like to."

"Nor will this be, when the time is right." He kissed her eyes, brushing her lashes with his lips. Then pulling her head back with a gentle tug, he traced the line of her throat with his lips, his tongue touching lightly in the hollow of her throat. His breath was hot against her flesh as he cupped her breast in his palm and his quick suckling kiss soothed her swollen nipple. Before her indrawn breath was released, he was closing her blouse.

Her breasts thrust against the silken fabric, a drop of moisture darkening it. The mark of his kiss. With a finger, he traced the tiny circle, caressing her softness beneath. In the diner, he had branded her as Slade's woman. Now he had done so again.

His hand fell away. Was he lying to himself? Was he so desperate for her that he would justify anything? Had he made a mistake weeks ago when he would not let her leave? No, he answered his own doubts. If there was a mistake, it was only his lust for her. None of the rest was wrong. Not the realization of her dreams or her blossoming into the woman she was meant to be. Yet Beth would never quite be that woman, nor could her dreams be fulfilled. Not until she was completely free of the past.

She could never truly be Slade's woman, but she could be free. "One day," he promised, "I'll set you free." Oblivious of her bewildered look, he caught her hand in his, saying, "There's no more we can do here today. Let's go home."

Seven

————

Hunter paused in the doorway of The Morning Glory Boutique. As always, he felt a sense of pride. Word of Beth and the opportunity she provided local craftsmen had spread like wildfire from mountaintop to hidden cove. As Hunter predicted, there was no shortage of offerings to stock the boutique. Boutique, gallery, neither was the proper name for a shop with such uniquely varied merchandise, but he couldn't think of a better one.

In displaying her wares, Beth revealed a unique artistry. Woven baskets were not stacked helter-skelter but tucked within a length of bright, rough, woven fabric and scattered with polished river stones. Turquoise jewelry, some simple, some ornate, was draped over the gracefully twisting coils of a weathered tree branch. A blown-glass decanter looked perfectly at home perched on a jagged, moss-covered stone. Ordinary objects entrusted to Beth became unique, enticing browsers to buy.

The shop was a canvas waiting for her touch.

"Hunter! Come look!"

Beth. He smiled and stepped farther into the empty shop. It was always the same. When he came to take her home, she treated his arrival as the focal point of her life.

"Come look!" she said again, her enthusiasm as new and fresh as when the shop had opened nearly a month ago. "There's someone I want you to meet."

The shop was not deserted as he thought. A tall, slender girl with rippling hair as black as his own stood in the shadows beyond the muted lights of a display case.

"Raven McCandless," the woman said as she stepped forward. Her hand was rough and dry, her fingers strong as she shook his hand. "I've heard a great deal about you and your work."

"And I yours," Hunter acknowledged.

"I doubt that." Her laugh was low, the burr of Scotland in her voice. At first glance, she seemed barely out of her teens, but tiny laugh lines that crinkled about brilliant blue-gray eyes attested to a few years more.

"I know your pottery is incomparable and that it's never been for sale. We have mutual friends. I've seen your gifts to them and your rare exhibits at the Folk Art Center."

At Hunter's comment, Beth turned to Raven. "You've never sold your work?"

"Never before," Raven amended.

"Why now? Why this shop? Why me?" Beth realized she was sputtering and forced herself to stop.

"This is why." Raven McCandless flicked a switch and a darkened showcase was flooded with muted light, revealing an astonishing array of pottery. Some were engraved, some painted. Some were graceful, some heavy and starkly arresting. They were black and sienna, shades of beige and red and of purest white. All bore the flowering dogwood, Raven's signature. All were arranged with the flair that was becoming Beth's unwritten signature.

"I still don't understand," Beth said.

"I do." Hunter spoke before Raven. "You've taken each item entrusted to you and treated it as something special. These aren't just simple mountain crafts, they're works of art. You've known it instinctively." He touched a delicate urn. "If someone wanted to buy 'this cute little pot,' would you sell it?"

"In that tone and attitude, no, I wouldn't."

Hunter smiled. "I rest my case. Raven," he said, addressing the quiet woman who nodded her head in agreement, "I was about to take Beth to dinner. Would you care to join us?"

"Another time." Raven smiled again, easily, as comfortable with them as if she'd known them for years. "It's late and I have an hour's drive down the mountain. Beth." She took Beth's hand in an arresting combination of serenity and old-fashioned gentility. Her clasp was strong and quick. "Hunter." Her hand met his in that quick clasp. "I've seen your work. It's good to meet you at last. I've read of your exhibit in Brighton. Good luck with it. And to you, Beth, with the boutique."

At the snap of her fingers, two Doberman pinschers, huge even for their breed, rose from the shadows and padded after her. With a final wave of goodbye, Raven made her way past scattered racks and cases. Her spine was straight, her steps measured, her hair flowed down her back in a fall of ebony.

The tinkling bell over the door was silent before Hunter whistled softly. "Do you realize what you've done?"

"What I've done?" Beth gave him a startled glance. In her worry that she'd made a terrible blunder, she forgot to question Hunter about Brighton.

"You've done what no one else in the world could do. Raven McCandless has never consented to offer her work for sale."

Beth gestured toward the magnificent arrangement in the lighted case. "She isn't a potter by trade?"

"No. I've heard she teaches at a community college and has written several books on wildflowers. Until now, she's been adamant in keeping her pottery for her own amusement."

"Then why has she changed now?"

"Since I know her only by reputation, I can only speculate that you truly are her reason. Beyond that, who knows? At any rate, this calls for a celebration. But first—" he kissed her startled mouth "—I have a gift for you."

It was always a shock to Beth that Hunter could move swiftly without seeming to hurry. Because he was so agile, it was easy to forget that he towered over everyone. When he returned to the shop, her gaze was drawn more to the lithe play of muscles rippling under the weight of a paper-wrapped box he carried than to the box itself. She wondered if he had modeled any of his sculptures after himself.

No, she decided. He had no idea what a beautiful man he was, no concept of the perfection of his body. It was a pity, for she would've wanted such a likeness to take with her when the time came for her to leave. *Time to leave!* Beth realized she hadn't thought about leaving in a long, long while.

"Are you going to stand there staring at me, or would you like to open this?" Hunter was laughing as he set the long, flat box on the floor.

Beth sank to her knees beside him, aware of his clean scent, the music of his laughter, his kindness. The box was not a box at all, she discovered and Hunter's infectious

mood left no room for gloom as she tore the paper away
from the object it hid.

Drawing back, she stared reverently at morning glories
carved so perfectly in gray, weathered wood that their
blooms looked to be of velvet rather than oak. A single
hummingbird flitted among vines that twined about graceful letters. A sign—Hunter's contribution to The Morning
Glory Boutique. One of a countless number to her life.

"It's beautiful." Her wandering fingers traced lines and
curves that flowed with the grain of the wood. "I don't deserve this."

"Yes, you do."

"No."

"Yes." Hunter caught both her hands in his.

"I can't repay you."

"Yes, you can. Just smile and say thank-you."

Beth turned, tearing herself away from the gentle darkness of his eyes. She looked about her, lingering long on
every facet of the room, proof of Hunter's belief in her. She
looked down at his hands holding hers. Hands of a man
who was strong and generous. Who gave her a dream, asking nothing in return. If he believed so strongly, could she
do less? When she looked into his face, she found him
waiting. With the last of her doubt gone, she murmured the
thanks she knew he truly did not want.

"My pleasure," he responded. Cupping her hands to his
face, Hunter kissed her palms. Releasing her, he rose.

Twilight had fallen as the sun sank below the mountains.
It was the time when the world hung suspended between day
and night and lights seemed oddly inefficient. Hunter
looked down at her, crouched in the gathering shadows, her
hair gleaming in the meager light like molten gold. He
waited until her face lifted to him, until the mass of her hair

swung like a curtain over her shoulder. He offered his hand and called her name, and waited once more.

He should have been no more than a hulking specter looming over her with the light at his back, but Beth saw him as clearly as if it were midday. All that he was, the essence of him, was there. In the tilt of his head. In the melodic tone of his voice. In the hand that waited for hers.

Beth smiled up at him, wondering how she could ever leave him. Her hand sought his, her fingers twining like the morning glories through his. As she rose to stand by the side of the man she loved, she realized with sudden clarity that the decision was no longer hers. Hunter might never love her, but if she left him, the choice would be his.

"Ready?"

"The sign!"

"We'll hang it tomorrow when the light's better."

"Of course," Beth agreed, and with her hand still in his, she followed him from The Morning Glory Boutique.

Hunter was restless. He'd paced the floor of the studio like a caged panther since he'd left Beth. Leaving her each night after dinner and walking the rocky path to what had become a virtual torture chamber was difficult. Tonight was a true test of his strength. Even now, he saw her kneeling in a pool of light, surrounded by the ambience of the boutique, her face lifted to his. And in her eyes, the look he had waited so long to see.

He would not fool himself that it was the look of love. He knew he could never expect love. Nor was it the gratitude he would never want. He had seen peace and the absence of fear.

"For the first time, she looked at me without that haunted look in her eyes and it sends me into a tailspin like a rutting stag." He spoke in a low snarl. "She's finally shaking free of one man, and I want to..."

He paced the length of the room again, knowing as he did that the little trek would end on the terrace. In its tenebrous shelter, he could stare up at the house, undetected, imagining that she was there at her window, perhaps looking down as he looked up.

He closed his burning eyes. He had work to do. It would not wait while he bayed at the moon in the throes of lust. The exhibit of his sculptures was scheduled at the Coastal Museum of Brighton in less than two weeks. Some of his work had been shipped overland to the North Carolina coast already. Some had not. He had never been as lax or as negligent. At least, he reminded himself wryly, it was only the smaller, easily transported pieces that were left.

The showing of his work was a necessary evil. Though he never participated in the social activity that surrounded such events, he always took charge of installing the exhibit. Then he would disappear to nurse his own private fears. "Perhaps we have more in common than you know," he muttered to the golden-haired woman who was always in his thoughts.

The library light blinked on in the house above. Hunter wondered if Beth was too restless to sleep and searched for something to read. A bitterness he'd learned to live with but never conquered twisted his face into a grim smile.

Something to read; the gift denied him.

After the light was extinguished, Hunter stood listening to the call of an owl, letting a breeze of the mountain night cool his fevered flesh. There was a tinge of fall in the air. Soon, the late-flowering morning glories would bloom by the waterfall. Then Beth would no longer be bound by her promise. She would be free to go. Maybe, he thought, it was for the best.

With heavy footsteps, Hunter returned to his studio. H
was working with a single-minded determination when he
tap sounded at his door. The hour was of little conse
quence, but he knew instinctively that in an evening tha
stretched endlessly before him, it was still barely past mid
night. The sweat of his labor had eased his fevered body, bu
beneath the chill, he felt a flush of rising heat like wildfire
The calm he'd courted deserted him as Beth waited beyon
the door.

Setting aside a figure that would be listed in the inven
tory of the show, he hesitated only a moment, then went t
admit her. "Beth," he said, stepping aside. "Come in." Sh
was dressed in jeans and chambray shirt and was enchant
ingly disheveled. Though her scrubbed face was drawn an
weary, Hunter saw beauty. "Is something wrong?"

"I couldn't sleep. I found this in the book I was read
ing." She offered an unopened letter with a recent post
mark. "Your lights were on, so I brought it down." He
color heightened under his hard stare. He hadn't onc
looked at the letter. "I suppose it could've waited until to
morrow, but I thought it might be important."

This was new territory for her. With the layman's curi
osity in the artist's sanctum, she looked about the studio a
the obvious turmoil of Hunter's packing. "You were busy.'
Laying the letter on a table, she turned to go. "I'm sorry
interrupted."

"No." Hunter said the word more loudly than he in
tended. "There's very little left to do. Stay. Please."

"Wouldn't you prefer to read your letter in private?"

"No. I don't want to read my letter."

"But it might be—"

"Something important," he finished for her. "You'r
beginning to sound like a broken record. If the damn lette
bothers you so much, then you read it."

Beth had never been inside the studio. She had waited for an invitation that never came. Now she had intruded. She could understand if he was too preoccupied to accept her interruption with great grace, but this was not like Hunter. His mouth was twisted into an ugly smile, his glare hard and fierce. There was anger in him, and a strange fervor. Yet his face was so pallid beneath its copper hue that she feared he was ill.

Beth sighed, admitting to herself that the letter was only an excuse to be with him. After their encounter in the boutique, she was puzzled by his brusque withdrawal immediately following dinner. He'd eaten with little appetite, yet had given no inkling of ill health. If he didn't feel well, naturally he wanted to be alone to rest.

She moved to leave, but hesitated, finding she couldn't. Without realizing it, she parroted his own worried concern. "Is something wrong?"

"Nothing's wrong, Beth. Just read the damn letter."

"All right." Still not convinced, she tore open the letter and read it. After a time, she looked up. "You have a show?" A look of sudden comprehension crossed her face. "The show Raven mentioned—in Brighton."

Hunter only nodded.

"I didn't know! I've kept you from your work with my problems and the boutique. That's why you rarely sleep."

If she knew he was not sleeping, then neither was she. Hunter was troubled by the revelation but let it slide. "You haven't kept me from anything crucial. This is an exhibit of an old series, nothing new."

"This letter asks you to reconsider your decision not to attend the opening."

"I won't be reconsidering."

"Because of me? Of Eric?"

"It has nothing to do with either of you. I'll see to the arranging of the pieces, as usual, but no more. While I'm gone, Zachary and Nathan will look after you."

"But you won't attend the opening?"

"No."

In her years with Eric, one lesson Beth learned was the value of public relations. From the tone of the letter, this was an important occasion. Possibly the most important in Hunter's career. "How can you not go? It could mean a great deal to you."

"That changes nothing."

"Why, Hunter?" She took a step forward, her hand rested on his arm. She looked up at him, confounded and confused. If she thought his eyes were fierce before, now she saw hot, naked savagery in them. The look he gave her shook her to the core, but she refused to back away. "These people are interested in Hunter, the sculptor. They won't give a thought to your background. So what earthly reason can you have for refusing?"

"What reason?" Hunter did not move away. His brawny body towered over her, yet oddly, he withdrew. The incandescence drained from his eyes, the intensity from his manner. Only his pallor was unchanged. When he finally spoke, his voice was like notes from a minor key, haunting and mournful. "Why don't you ask why I didn't read the letter or why I don't read the newspaper? Haven't you wondered why the books in the library are in mint condition? Have you seen me read instructions or write down a message? Have you never considered why Archer called me 'dummy'?" He flung her hand from his arm. "Dammit, Beth! Are you blind?"

Now it was Beth's face that was pallid. She felt the color drain from it. Her eyes were blue pools of shock as she remembered menus never read, books cradled like treasures, but whose pages did not turn. She heard Minnie Jenkins's voice damning him for refusing to learn, Archer's calling him dummy. She heard, too, Hunter's own words.

The last man who called me that...

Her body trembled, not in fear but in agony for this proud man who had borne too much. He was not illiterate. He was too intelligent, too informed. His library spoke of a man who loved books. Had he been holding one when the letter came? The letter he could not read, tucked into a book he could not read.

"Dyslexia." The word was a raw, aching whisper as she understood. Dyslexia, one more strike against an innocent child, making his isolation complete.

"Hunter the dummy half-breed can't read," he said softly, and Beth heard the echo of a thousand jeers.

"Dyslexia can be overcome. Schools have—"

"Most schools. Most dyslexia," he said bluntly. "But not Hunter Slade's. Nobody understood about dyslexia. It wasn't your common, everyday, household word here thirty years ago. It wouldn't have mattered if it had been. There's a rare form that's not overcome just once, it must be overcome everyday." He sighed, weary with the probing of old wounds. "Every day is like the first day. What I learn today, I have to relearn tomorrow. There aren't enough hours in a day, or a lifetime."

"You made so sure I knew everything the gossips might tell me about you. But not this. Did you think it would matter?"

"That I'm defective?" His words were labored, drawn from his private purgatory. "Yes!" Suddenly, violently angry at the world, at himself, at her, he spat out, "Yes, I thought it would matter."

"Defective!" Beth drew back as if she'd been struck. The word sickened her. "You thought that little of me?" she whispered. "That it would change how I feel about you?"

"Doesn't it?"

Beth was suddenly seized by calm fury. "Yes," she responded in a voice empty of emotion. "I suppose it does. It proves you aren't the man I thought you were—hoped you were."

Hunter had half turned from her. Now, he swung about, his head thrown back, his black hair flying. His eyes glittered with a bitter light.

Before he could speak, Beth continued in a tone that at first seemed conversational, then as he listened, it sent shivers down his spine. "I needed a friend," she began her litany. "I thought I found one. I needed for someone to see value in me. I thought you did. I wanted to be more than a decoration. I thought, for you, I was. Now I see that it was all a mistake. You saw no more in me than the rest of the world.

"I'm a face and a body, but never, ever, a woman with a mind and a heart. Who feels compassion. Who understands and hurts for someone she cares for.

"And all the time, I thought . . . I thought . . ." She swallowed back tears that would have burned like acid if she let them fall. She swayed on her feet. With her fingertips pressing into her temples in an effort to drive away the pain thundering in her head, she drew a long, deep breath. Slowly, her head came up. Her eyes were dry and cold as glaciers. "It's what you thought that matters, isn't it?"

Hunter said nothing to confirm or deny her words.

"I won't make light of your disability. It must be devastating. But the issue isn't dyslexia. It wouldn't matter to me if you read six languages or a hundred or none! Or if I'd never known at all." Her face was etched with despair. "I didn't mean to pry. And if I pushed when I shouldn't, I'm sorry. Not dyslexia, nor anything you've ever said or done has made me think less of you.

"What there is between us, 'the magic,' you called it, is based on trust." Beth bowed her head, filled with the grief of disillusionment. "Or so I thought," she whispered. "Without benefit of doubt, you judged and found me lacking. Given your history, your sense of honor, I would've expected better.

"That was my first mistake. The second was coming here tonight." Beth moved to the door, her shoulders tensed, waiting for the lash of his retaliation. Only the soft brush of her steps over the quarry stone followed her. At the open doorway, she paused, her back to him, one hand on the wooden frame. "For the record," she said in a husky voice, "your mistake was in deciding this is important beyond its hurt to you."

"I can't read, Beth."

"I betrayed myself for wealth and position."

"It's not the same thing."

"No, it isn't, is it? I had a choice. You didn't. Now which of us would you say is the defective one?"

"Beth! Don't!"

"It's an ugly word, isn't it? Can you imagine how sick it makes me to hear the finest man I've ever met call himself..." Beth stopped. She had no idea Hunter had crossed the room to her until his hands came down on her shoulders.

"The finest?" he said with a surprised laugh. "A moment ago, you called me an arrogant bastard."

"I didn't! I wouldn't."

"Not in those exact words, but the meaning was the same. You were right. I am."

"Don't!"

He turned her to face him, his fingers gently massaging the tense muscles of her shoulders. With a quirk of a sooty black eyebrow, he asked softly, "Defending me against myself again?"

Beth felt herself falling into the dark depths of his midnight eyes. Her anger evaporated beneath the skipping beat of her heart. Breathlessly, she murmured, "Somebody has to. You can handle the world with one hand tied behind you, but you have no defenses against your worst enemy."

"Myself?"

"Yes."

"I have you." The words were a low breath. Before Beth could respond, his hand cupped her chin, his thumb teasing lightly over her lips, back and forth in a mesmeric rhythm. His gaze held hers; his scent enveloped her. Back and forth, sensual, undemanding, yet as captivating as if he'd bound her. His thumb grew still. His eyes closed. With a ragged groan, he drew her against him. "Tiger lady," he murmured, "what am I going to do with you?"

Beth had no answer. She was content to bask in his embrace, to let life be no more than the strong heart beating beneath her cheek. Here, there was no prejudice, no failure. Hurts and mistrust were forgotten. There was little more she could ask.

Hunter's embrace tightened. His lips brushed over her hair. His breath teased her skin. "You make a man believe he can do anything. One smile from you and I look for dragons to slay, good deeds to do. All in hope of winning a second smile. I watched the truckers. They flirted and teased, but there wasn't a man among them who wouldn't walk through fire for you. As I would."

He took a step back. Their bodies no longer touched, but he did not release her. "What penance for my transgressions? Good deed or dragon? The choice is yours."

"There's no need—"

"Deed or dragon?"

"Don't be ridiculous," Beth said with a laugh, marveling at how quickly they had gone from somber to light-hearted.

"What deed, tiger lady?"

Beth thought a moment, then sighed. "You've done so much already, I can't think of another thing."

"What dragon?"

The smile slipped from her face. The game had suddenly ended for her. She regarded him solemnly. "Your own."

"That would make you happiest, wouldn't it? If I could shake free of my inhibitions and be the man you hoped I was."

Mortified, Beth recalled her accusation, flung at him in hurt and anger. Words she could deny but not recall. "The man you already are," she insisted.

"But for one last dragon," Hunter mused almost absently. His hands moved restlessly down the length of her arm and back again. His thoughts were in a land that no one but Hunter walked. His chest rose; a breath was drawn deeply, held, then slowly released. "I'll go."

"Go?" Her mind raced to catch up with his.

"To Brighton," he said so calmly, no one but Beth would guess that he'd just slain the fiercest dragon of all and laid it at her feet.

"Hunter. I didn't understand. No one could ask that much of you."

"I've asked you to stand and fight for what you want. To challenge Eric from the security of your dreams. Can I do less?"

"How will you manage?"

"I'll memorize what I need to, as I always have. If there's something unexpected—" He shrugged, but the nonchalance was not quite believable. Beth knew, then, it was the unexpected he feared. She suspected it was the flaw in the dyslexic's armor. "I'll do as always," he said. "Avoid it."

"And if you can't?"

He shrugged again, no more successfully.

Beth knew little of dyslexia, but she was no stranger to humiliation. Eric had seen to that. Hunter needn't feel its sting, not while she could help. "I'm going with you."

"I can't let you do that."

"You can't stop me." Beth lifted her chin, daring him to challenge her decision. "Wherever you go, I'll never be more than a step away. Call me your secretary or your maid. Call me anything or nothing. As you like, but I'll be there."

"What about the boutique? Is it wise to leave it?"

"Leaving is no problem." Her mind was racing, outstripping her words. She had the logical choice—no, better than that. The perfect choice. "Raven!"

"Raven McCandless?"

"Raven is such a common name, there's another around?" Beth laughed. "Of course, Raven McCandless. We had an instant rapport. I know she'll do it. Maybe better than I."

"You're certain?"

"So certain that all that's left is to ask." She indicated his telephone. "May I?"

"Honey—" Hunter chuckled at finding himself caught up in her enthusiasm "—it's past midnight. Don't you think it could wait until tomorrow?"

"Well..." She cast a sorrowful eye at the gleaming instrument. "If you insist."

"I insist. Now, in deference again to the hour and to these—" he drew his fingertips gently over the shadows beneath her eyes "—I think I should walk you back to the house. Tomorrow I'll contact Marlee Adamson. She's a friend and the moving force behind this show. She's repeatedly offered the use of her home, as well, for as long as I need it."

"Won't she resent my intrusion?"

"Never. She's a warm, generous woman who loves company. One more guest is one more delight. She'll love you at first sight. Now," he said sternly, "it's time you were in bed." With a gallant gesture that allowed no resistance, he led her through the open doorway. And all the while, his heart and body wanted only to keep her.

Eight

Hunter looked about the museum gallery. For the first time, he was alone. Only a few patrons still wandered through the premier showing of his work. Tugging at his tie, he swung about, searching for Beth. It was a purely reflexive act, for during the course of the evening, in the few times she had been drawn from his side, he discovered she would find him if he needed her.

There. Her eyes met his in a private smile as she listened to the animated conversation of Marlee Adamson. Hunter relaxed, savoring the pleasure he found in watching Beth.

She wore a dress of coarse homespun trimmed with lace of a slightly darker shade of cream. Its simple lines skimmed her body, yet the low-cut, lace-filled bodice with its trim of unpolished turquoise never let one forget the lush curves beneath. Belled sleeves caught back by a single turquoise button revealed more lace. She was a stunning creation of peaches and cream and gold and blue. No man in the room could keep his eyes from her.

A plump woman heavily weighted by diamonds positioned herself imperiously before him. "I must have this one." She waved a beringed hand at an ebony figure. "I simply must."

Hunter inclined his head gallantly, lessening the sting of his refusal. "*Winter Morning* is not for sale."

"Everything is for sale, for a price. Name it."

"Perhaps in most cases, but *Winter Morning* is priceless. Not to me, to the owner of that particular collection." He drew comfort from Beth's hand sliding through the crook of his arm as he explained. "It was lent to the museum by Zachary Steele. There is but one of each. No other castings have been done. The model in each is his wife, Christen. Each piece has a special meaning."

"I must have just the one."

"No, Alycia. What you must do is commission a piece of your own." Marlee Adamson had arrived in the midst of the conversation. She was startlingly tiny, but she wielded a big stick in Brighton society. "This is an exhibit, not a sale."

"But . . ." the woman sputtered.

"There are no buts." Marlee rested her hand on Beth's, where it clasped Hunter's arm. "Beth has voiced a desire to see the barrier islands by moonlight. They've barely time to make a dash for the house to change before the light fails. Hunter knows the channels and the buoys well enough, but it's easier in twilight." She turned her back on the larger woman, dismissing her. "Now, children," she whispered, "run! While you have the chance."

"God bless you." Hunter laughed and bent to kiss her.

"No. God bless you for sharing yourself and your talent with us at last. Now go! You've done your duty for this day. I'll see you tomorrow. But mind you, not too early."

Casually, Beth and Hunter worked their way to the door. Once there, like children escaping the classroom, they dashed down the street to the parked Mercedes.

"So this was what you and Marlee had your heads together about this morning," Hunter said as he settled behind the wheel.

"Not me. Marlee. She gets the credit. She said you loved sailing almost as much as Zachary." Beth touched his wrist beneath the cuff of his shirt. "Is there no end to your talents?"

"Flattery, my dear?" He wagged a teasing eyebrow.

"Truth." Beth sobered. "There is only that between us."

"Always." Hunter lifted her hand and kissed her fingers. "Now, how about dinner?"

"All taken care of."

"Marlee?"

"Of course. She says all we need to do is get ourselves and the little we will need for the night to the boat."

"Marlee's a terrific lady."

"She seems as fond of Zachary as she is of you."

"Zachary knew her first. He was born in Brighton. He clawed his way out of the waterfront slums and by way of Vietnam, into medicine. He studied and served his residency here. Christen was in the same program. They were friends and, for a brief time, more than friends. Then something went wrong. Christen left the hospital and returned to Laurenceville. Zachary completed his residency and set up an office in Brighton."

"He met Marlee then," Beth surmised.

"She became his patient. He became her pupil. She smoothed down the rough edges and taught him the social graces. I'm sure you can imagine that no one sends Zachary anywhere, and he came to Laurenceville for a lot of reasons. One was to spend his sabbatical working in the clinic while Nathan was away recuperating from a serious illness. The most important reason was Christen. Yet, somehow, I suspect Marlee had a subtle hand in it. Whoever's responsible, Zachary came to Laurenceville. Time and Marlee's polish had mellowed him. Christen had changed, too. She was a confident woman with the strength to understand and love him.

"His bitterness toward her was no match for the woman she'd become. He fell in love with her all over again."

"He came and he stayed?" Beth asked.

"Not at first. There's no instant cure for stubbornness like Zachary's. He returned to Brighton and resumed his practice, determined to forget her. His collection of my sculptures of her and his own heart wouldn't let him."

"Your sculptures! Was Marlee responsible for his discovering them?"

"A knowledge of art was included in the refinement of Zachary Steele. It was sheer coincidence that he stumbled across my work. But coincidence had nothing to do with his recognition of Christen or with his becoming a collector."

Beth understood. "As beautiful as they are, stone and bronze and terra-cotta were a poor substitute for flesh and blood. For the real Christen."

"Exactly. He came back to Laurenceville, for Christen. This time, he stayed. Now she's happier than I've ever seen her. Marlee's partly responsible, and I'm grateful."

"That's why you agreed to do this exhibit, isn't it? But not to appear."

"Marlee didn't ask that. She wouldn't."

Beth looked at Hunter. By choice, he had few friends. Those he chose were rare and special. As he was.

Hunter lapsed into silence. His mind turned to the quiet woman beside him and the problems the evening ahead could present for her. "Beth," he said, breaking into her thoughts. "If we take the boat out this late, it would be safest to anchor off shore for the night." He looked at her leaving the remainder of his question unasked.

"Then we'll do what's safest," she said simply.

"You're sure?" he asked huskily.

Beth bowed her head. For the space of a heartbeat, she was still, her face hidden by hair that fell like a curtain over her cheek. Then, sweeping it back with her hand, she returned his look with utter calm. He saw her smile and heard her lovely voice saying, "I've never been more sure of anything in my life."

Hunter had no words or any voice to speak them. He simply took her hand in his.

"Who would believe it?"

Hunter was surprised by the sound of his own voice, but no more than by the events of the past week. One day, he'd been making final preparations for the show in Brighton. Two days later, it was history and he was in the middle of the Atlantic aboard the *Lady Christen,* Zachary's magnificent single-masted sloop. Well, he confessed, if not the middle the Atlantic at least.

And talking to himself.

He smiled at the specific postscript. With a what-the-hell shrug, he slid down in his seat, propped his feet on a rail and folded his hands over his middle. Lazily, he looked out at a world that bore little resemblance to Laurenceville. Actually, beyond the star-studded sky that stretched into forever, there was decidedly no resemblance.

To his right lay miles of calm, empty sea. To his left, a deserted barrier island with sands glistening like snow under the September moon. In Laurenceville, autumn colors were subtly drifting through woodland and field. Green was laced with amber and scarlet, and morning glories soon would bloom by the waterfall. Here, where coastal North Carolina glided into South, summer held the land in thrall.

A full moon hung like a flaming ball over a shimmering sea. A salt-laden breeze waxed and waned. The drowsy murmuring of breakers sweeping a distant shore sang softly of long summer days and deep purple nights.

From the depths of indolence, he marveled at his sense of tranquility. He wondered if he'd contracted a touch of moon madness, then decided no. He suffered from a totally different malady. Contentment. Bone deep and gratifying. With the world, with this night, with himself. It was a good feeling, a rare one. And he owed it all to...

"Beth." He finished his thought aloud as he watched her step onto the deck from the galley below. She approached in a surefooted glide that hinted of years on the open sea. Yet Beth was a novice as he had been when Zachary had accepted Hunter's total ignorance of sailing as a challenge. During parts of two summers spent as Marlee's house-guests, with dogged patience on Zachary's part and iron-clad endurance on Hunter's, Hunter had become a better-than-average sailor. Nothing to rival Zachary, who had grown up on the waterfront of Brighton and was sailing by the time he was strong enough to handle the rigging, yet more than capable of captaining Zachary's prized *Lady* through the maze of islands.

As he admired Beth's bare midriff beneath the knotted tails of her golden shirt and the length of shapely legs flashing beneath snug, white shorts, he asked himself if any captain ever had a more alluring first mate.

"You seemed preoccupied." Her voice was a muted sound in the deep blue cocoon of sea and sky.

"Just wool-gathering. Come keep me company."

"That was my original intention."

Hunter glanced at the sky, at the path the moon traveled. "You were belowdecks a long time. Are you all right?"

"Am I seasick? Not a twinge. I don't know the nautical terms for it," she said with a smile, "but in landlubber's language, the galley's in order."

"I could've helped."

"Nope." She shook her head adamantly as she set a glass of sparkling grape juice beside him. Christen's gift, sent in lieu of champagne, anticipating an evening such as this. "This is your special night. Nothing as mundane as returning a few items to their proper places and repacking a picnic basket should besmirch it."

"'Besmirch'?" Hunter raised a lazy eyebrow.

Beth laughed and sat beside him. "It's a perfectly good word."

"It was a good exhibit."

"Good!" Beth chortled and rested the tip of a sneaker-clad foot by Hunter's on the coaming. "You're a master of understatement. It was a spectacular night! You were wonderful. Your work speaks for itself, but tonight, you added charisma to the mystique. I eavesdropped shamelessly. The men were intrigued by the reclusive, never-photographed Hunter Slade, and the women? Well, you sexy devil, just take your choice."

"Ha!" Hunter dismissed her plaudit. "Sounds more as if you've been listening to Marlee. She likes men and makes no bones about it. She enjoys playing fairy godmother to us. Now that Zachary's life is an unqualified success, she's taken my career as her next project."

"You could do worse. She was the moving force behind this showing. She made it the success it was."

Hunter drew her hand to his chest. "You made it a success. You were my talisman."

"I wouldn't have been anywhere else," Beth declared. "But there was never a time beyond your control. You didn't need me."

"I needed you." Hunter's voice was as hushed as the distant surf. He lifted her palm to his lips. Folding her hand in both of his he murmured, "I need you now."

They had lived in a time of grace, now the look in his eyes foretold its end. Banked fires blazed beneath contentment. Smoldering desire hovered on the brink of conflagration. Yet his very stillness offered choice. Beth tore her gaze from his. Her thoughts riveted on his hands. They were the gateway to his heart. When fate would make him mute, through them he spoke to the world. No word, written or read, could express as much as Hunter's hands.

From this night forward, her life would be in those beautiful hands. That was her choice.

Slipping free of his grasp, she rose to her feet. With her palm still tingling from his kiss, she cupped his cheek. His skin burned with the heat of the night. Her own burned with a need the ocean's breeze could never cool.

The island beckoned; white sands invited. "Please." It was a single word spoken from her heart. She waited until he stood, rising slowly to his great height. His contentment had fled; his stare was fierce and wild. He made no move to touch her, but he throbbed with an intensity Beth knew only she could ease. Slipping her hand about his neck, she drew his mouth to hers. Her kiss was gentle, but her lingering lips made sweet promises. Once more, softly entreating, she murmured, "Please."

Then she was gone. In a flash of long, tanned legs, she was over the side. Her body sliced the diamond-bright water, disappearing beneath the reflection of countless moons. Hunter searched the unbroken, shimmering surface, hearing only the splash of the rippling sea against the side of the sloop.

Beth surfaced. Tossing her soaked hair from her face, she began to swim toward shore. Hunter smiled, watching the graceful arc of her stroke. His shirt was closed by a single button. With a flick of his finger and a shrug of his shoulders, the shirt slid from his body. He'd barely kicked free of his shoes before he knifed through the water as cleanly as Beth.

His dive was deeper, farther. His powerful stroke longer, quicker. When he reached shallow water, the peaceful shore was deserted. He turned, scanning the water. Once more, only the rustling of the tide disturbed its mirrored surface.

Then Beth was rising from the surf with her head flung back exultantly, water cascading like liquid jewels down her body. She stood in the spindrift, eyes darkened to turquoise holding his. The knot of her golden shirt was untied, the buttons open, the length of it clinging like a caress. Beneath moonlight that rivaled day, the thrust of her breasts was revealed; the darkening of an impudent nipple; the curve of a tawny hip. Beyond her shirt she wore nothing, the rest of her clothing cast adrift in the sea.

No garment would ever become her more than moonlight. If he could sculpt a dream, it would be this. Beth, proud, regal, golden. And so beautiful, she took his breath away.

This was no dream. She was flesh and blood, this woman who approached, one graceful, deliberate step following another. She was honor and fierce loyalty. She was desire.

She stopped before him, her arms at her side, her face raised to his. Only the uneven tempo of her breathing betrayed her agitation. He touched her lips in the gentlest of kisses. Then with a groan, he drew her hard against him, molding her body to his. His kiss grew wild. His arms were

steel bands about her. There was no contentment in him, nor
gentleness. His voice was hushed, filled with his own aching need. "Sweet Beth, I've thought of nothing but you
since the moment I first saw you. I wanted you then. I want
you now."

Beth stepped out of his embrace. "I know." She brushed
a strand of damp hair from his face. "This was the magic
between us."

She took his hand, leading the way to shore. Beyond the
water's edge, she turned, sliding her shirt from her body,
casting it away with a careless hand, barely aware that it
fluttered about her feet. Hunter reached for her. Only Beth's
subtle gesture of denial stopped him. "First this," she said,
her hands going to the rope tied at the waist of his shorts.

Hunter stripped the offending clothing from him. In his
nakedness, from his heavy shoulders, down his lean, corded
torso to his muscled thighs, he was pure, raw power. With a
slashing impatience, he flung the single garment aside, taking the step needed to bring their bodies together. "Now,"
he said, almost harshly. "This."

His mouth came down on hers with a ferocity that was
nearly brutal. His hands slid down her back to the curving
swell of her buttocks, lifting her to him. His cradling body
was hard against hers. His chest rose and fell in short gasps
as her breasts teased him. The savage that lurked beneath
the civilized man was there, in the raw sensuality of each
caress, the urgency of his blatant desire.

No more savage or urgent than her own, Beth knew. With
swollen lips, she kissed the hollow of his throat, tasting the
salt left by the sea on her tongue. Sliding slowly from his
embrace, she nipped a tiny, virile nipple with sharp, white
teeth. Regaining her balance and ignoring the shudder that
shook him, she rose on tiptoe, her bareness molding once

more to his. Grasping his hair in both her hands as her lips parted eagerly to his hunger, she drew him down to the sand.

Hunter drew a deep, rasping breath, letting her lead him where she would. Matching kiss for kiss and embrace for embrace, he fought the quiet battle of restraint. Leaning over her, watching her respond to every touch, he accepted the gift of her passion. As a man, he learned the secrets of her body. As an artist, he worshiped its perfection.

This was madness, but as Beth writhed beneath him and cried out her need, Hunter knew there truly was magic in their madness. With an urgent cry of his own, his body covered hers, thrusting deeply, sheathing himself in clenching heat and moving in concert with her toward the ever-spiraling furor of mating. Even as they sought that deliverance, he wanted to prolong their search, to keep her with him as closely as this forever. But he had waited too long for her; his thirst was too great. The shuddering, keening madness was upon him.

Beth was with him. She matched his quickening pace until the magic was too powerful to contain. Her body cried out and was answered by his. In the exquisite, unthinking pleasure of fulfillment, she held him, shivering against him until the magic ended. Murmuring the promises of lovers, she subsided on a scrap of golden blouse that held back the sand.

The surf whispered, island breezes played about them and Hunter watched over Beth as she slept.

At dawn's first light, Hunter and Beth were strolling hand in hand over a shell-strewed shore. He wore shorts damp from the sea. Beth had tied her blouse sarong fashion about her waist.

Hunter found himself entranced all over again. She had given herself to him without reservation and in the aftermath, refused to hide behind the shield of false modesty. There was nothing brazen in the way she walked by his side. Baring her body before him was natural. With the resolving of her doubts, Beth became the most refreshingly honest woman Hunter had ever known.

"Look!" She knelt in the sand. "A starfish."

"I am looking," Hunter said in a rasping rumble.

"I know. You've been looking at me."

"Don't you know why?"

"Because you want me." She said it simply, without guile.

"Always." Lifting her to her feet, he slid his hands over her midriff. "There'll never be a moment in my life when I don't want you. It's more than want or need, it's because you're beautiful. Here." He caressed her breasts, watching as the nipples blossomed and darkened. "And especially here." He leaned to kiss the slope of her bosom where her heart beat.

Beth smiled up at him, her eyes shimmering. "No one ever told me I'm beautiful so beautifully."

Hunter threw back his head in a glorious roar of laughter. "Honey, I've never had anyone thank me so beautifully for the truth, or so often." Catching her about the waist, he pulled her to him, planting an exuberant kiss on her nose. "How would you like to go for a swim and we can—" He nipped her ear with his teeth and whispered his intentions.

"You can do *that* in the water?" Beth's skepticism was as real as it was in the spirit of the game.

Hunter nodded smugly. "Then you can thank me again."

"I can, huh? In that case, you're on." Rising on tiptoe, in one swift move, she brushed a kiss over his cheek and spun out of his embrace while pulling off her blouse. "If you can catch me."

Her discarded blouse fluttered about his face as she raced over the pink sands of dawn. Hunter was laughing as he untangled himself from her clothes and his own and sprinted after her.

Beth splashed through surf that reflected the scarlet of the rising sun and dived into it. Strafing the ocean's floor, she swam swiftly and with the pleasure gleaned from the years when swimming was the only outlet allowed for a young girl's energy. When Hunter grasped her ankle, she turned to him, more than willing to assist him in the water sport he suggested.

"Thank you," Hunter murmured.

"That was supposed to be my line."

"In my arrogance, I thought it was. Now I know it's mine."

"I would be arrogant."

"You would?"

"Certainly," Beth said soberly. "If I could carry you across the sand after that little exercise, I'd be arrogant."

"Careful there. You wouldn't want to be so generous with your backhanded praise that I dropped you."

"You wouldn't!"

"Wouldn't I?" But Hunter had no such intention. Instead, he laid her on the hard-packed sand and stretched out beside her.

"You didn't."

"Hush, woman." He curled himself about her, his chin resting on the top of her head. "Rest. You'll need your strength."

"I will?"

"Yes, you greedy child, for the swim to the boat."

"Oh."

"Is that disappointment I hear?"

"I hate to leave the island."

"I know." Hunter gathered her closer. "The sun will be fully risen soon, and Marlee will be waiting."

Beth turned in his arms. "We have a little time."

"Woman, you'll be the death of me yet." Hunter groaned and leaned to her, startling only himself in proving his feats of delight were not limited solely to the water.

The channel leading to Marlee's creek house was deserted when Hunter nosed the *Lady* to the dock and made her fast. The sun had nearly reached its meridian, and only the spreading oaks that shaded the rambling, Victorian cottage cast heavy shadows.

In helping Beth from the sloop, Hunter lifted her high, holding her above him, laughing up at her. He let her body slide down his, keenly aware of every rich curve, each secret part of her. "Good Lord, woman," he said when he could breathe again. "What do you do to me? I should be too exhausted for what I'm thinking."

Beth lifted an eyebrow and with lazy hands, combed her windblown hair with her fingers. With a wicked smile, she arched her back, drawing her emerald blouse taut over her breasts. The silky fabric did nothing to conceal her taut nipples.

"Tease!" He caught her by the waist, moving his body against hers in a slow, instinctive rhythm. "We haven't the time and this isn't the place, but I promise you, you have a debt to pay."

"Hold that thought," Beth said. "Until that time, here's a payment on my account." Her fingers burrowed in the thick pelt of his bare chest. Her mouth covered his, her tongue seeking entry. Her kiss was like a bolt of lightning slashing through her, transmitting its force to him. It didn't matter that they'd made love on the island, in the sea and on the deck of the *Lady*. Desire exploded between them as bold and fresh as if it were newborn.

"To hell with propriety!" Hunter growled as he seized the lapels of her blouse and ripped it open, sending the tiny buttons falling like raindrops of pearl. His hands covered her breasts; a proud, erect nipple nestled in each palm. "Marlee will have to wait. For now, we have better things to— What the devil?"

Hunter's head came up at an odd whirring sound. His first thought was to protect Beth. Pulling her to him, he covered her body with his. Over her shoulder, he glimpsed a figure slithering through the shadow of the oaks. Then he placed the sound. An automatic camera, recording their indiscretion.

Beth frowned up at him. "Who was that? What did he want?"

"I didn't get a good look at him, but I think I know."

"Who?" Beth asked in a quavering voice.

"A photojournalist with a score to settle. Last summer, when Zachary and I were here sailing, he wanted a story. 'Noble savage turns sculptor,' that sort of garbage. When I refused, he slithered about like a paparazzo."

"What did you do?"

"I wanted to break his nose, but settled for his camera."

"He has a new camera." Glumly she added, "And a story."

"Something catchy like, 'Noble savage takes a woman.'"

"Or Eric Weston's wife and the savage." Beth shuddered. "Whatever the title, once that picture hits the stands, Eric won't be far behind it."

"We've weathered storms before, we'll weather this one. I promised you long ago that if you stayed, I'd see that he never had you." Drawing back from her, Hunter tied the tails of her shirt beneath her breasts. It was his only choice, the buttons were scattered over the dock. His task done, he rested his hands on her hips. "Let's go inside and offer this problem to Marlee. Perhaps her fertile mind can offer a solution."

As Beth walked with him to Marlee's, the day, begun in a golden glow, was tarnished. The threat of Eric turned something lovely sordid. But only if we allow it, she thought suddenly. Only we can make it shameful. For a little while, Hunter loved me. No matter what happens, no matter what Eric does, nothing can take that away. Her fingers twined through Hunter's. When he smiled at her, the gold of the day was bright again.

"But my dears! The solution is obvious." Marlee looked from Beth to Hunter. "We can't keep that sleaze from publishing the story, but its sensationalism can be diffused. So can this dreary little man who's been bothering Beth."

"How?" Hunter and Beth asked in unison.

"With a marriage, of course." When her solution was greeted with shocked silence, she continued, "What's sensational about a man making love to his wife? If that photograph brings Eric running, he'll discover she's finally beyond his reach." Again Marlee's logic was met with silence. "How you feel about each other is clear. Why else do you think I arranged the cruise? Not even you could resist...." For the first time in nearly fifty years, Marlee blushed. "Well, could you?"

Hunter took Beth's hand in his. "The answer is obvious, isn't it?"

"Along with a good many other things," Marlee added dryly. "Beth, you haven't said a word. Do you love Hunter?"

"She cares for me," Hunter said before Beth could respond. "We would never have become lovers if she didn't."

"Then you care as much for her?" Marlee stressed Hunter's choice of words.

He lifted Beth's hand to his lips. "I've cared a great deal for a long time."

Beth opened her mouth to speak and found no words.

"Surely you've known, Beth. Why else would I break every rule of my life where you were concerned? Since Marlee's suggestion would be a solution, and considering that you know me very well, would you marry me?"

"What about Eric?" Beth asked in a daze.

"We'll handle him when the time comes. Together."

"Hunter..." Beth folded his hand in both of hers. "I—"

"My question requires only one word. Is your answer yes, Beth? Or is it no?"

Beth's gaze clung to his for an interminable time before turning to their clasped hands. His beautiful hands held her life in their palms. "Yes," she whispered. And then again, "Yes."

"Good!" Marlee cried. "We'll have the civil ceremony here as quickly as possible. Later, when you're home, I'm sure you'll want to observe the Cherokee—"

"Marlee!" Hunter's voice was like thunder, but his eyes never left Beth's face. "You've managed my career, my life, the seduction of my woman and my proposal. I think Beth and I can manage the rest."

The aged woman chuckled. "I thought you'd never get around to shooing me away."

"Consider yourself shooed." As the click of Marlee's heels faded down the hall, Hunter considered the day that would end Eric Weston's mad claim and the beginning of his own short time with Beth. Promising himself that he would protect her from the gambler, from the world, from himself, he said quietly in a voice that enchanted, "Shall we plan our wedding day? The day when you truly become Slade's woman."

Nine

"**W**ait." When Hunter spoke, Beth stopped, glancing u
curiously as he touched her arm. "We've discarded a lot c
customs in this marriage." He bent, swung her into his arm
and stepped over the threshold of his home. "This one
like."

Beth laughed and nuzzled his cheek. "Only this one?"

"I think, Mrs. Slade, that there are several customs
could grow very fond of, if we practiced them enough."

"Ahh, practice!" Beth linked her hands about his neck
exquisitely conscious of her breasts brushing against him i
rhythm with his walk. "Is that what you call it? Practice?"

"I'll do more than call it, if you don't watch it."

"Promises. Promises."

"Woman, you've got a big mouth."

"More to kiss," Beth said cheerfully, and raised he
mouth.

"Yeah." Hunter succumbed to her inducement. His arms tightened, his heart pounded in a meteoric rush. He was tempted to sink with her to the mat-strewed floor and lose himself in the rose-petal velvet of her body. Reason flickered like a candle in a whirlwind. Its cold light shattered romantic illusions that belonged to another time, another place. Where, for a while, he was another man.

Grief for that time, that man, lay like a cold, gray shroud over his spirit, driving the innocence from his Eden. With a deliberate effort, his lips released hers. His black gaze roved over the sun-warmed glow of her cheeks. Like a thirsting man, he drank in the sight of her mouth, swollen by his kisses. "Another time," he said in a despairing mutter. "Another place."

He pushed open the door to his bedroom and stepped inside. For a moment, his clasp tightened possessively. His chest rose and fell in a long, shuddering breath. Then slowly, his grip relaxed and he set her on her feet. The lilting laughter that spun itself like a gossamer thread through the days of their week-old marriage vanished. His voice was without inflection when he said, "You're home, Mrs. Slade."

With a flick of his finger the darkened room was awash with light. Beth was vaguely conscious of the subtle richness of color and line—the Spartan elegance of Hunter's masculinity; the expression of his talent. Absorbing her surroundings without seeing, she turned blindly to him, confused by the change in him. With the opening of a door, he was no longer the bronzed sailor who made love to her on the deck of the *Lady* by moonlight and on the sunlit shores of the island. The lover who renewed her faith in herself looked at her now through the brooding eyes of a stranger.

Beneath his alien stare, she was uncomfortably aware of her carelessly buttoned blouse, her bare breasts straining against its fabric. The natural sensuality born of touching and loving in complete trust seemed tawdry and she, a brazen seductress. What was beautiful with Hunter became ugly with this remote stranger.

Shame spread like a sickness. Shivering from a wintry chill, she turned away. Seeking a hiding place where there was none, she stood quietly before tall windows, wishing she could vanish into the deepening mountain shadows.

In bleak misery, Hunter's dark eyes consumed her, sweeping over the proud, straight back to the delicate curve of her hip. She gave herself to him completely. In her abandon, he learned to interpret every nuance, every mood. He knew her passion. He knew her stillness. And, as now, he knew when she struggled for composure.

His jaw rippled, his lip curled. Home less than five minutes and he'd already hurt her.

He hadn't meant for her to be touched by the bitter melancholy that deepened with each mile of their journey from the coast. But then—he grimaced in growing contempt—he hadn't meant so many things. He hadn't meant to become involved. He hadn't meant to be more than friend and protector. He hadn't meant to desire her so completely that passion ruled his head as well as his heart.

With no thought of the consequences, he had seized the treasure he coveted. His madness couldn't be undone, but he could offer her respite from his lust. "I'm sorry," he said to her back. "I wasn't thinking when I brought you here. You'll want to keep your own room, of course."

The shock of his suggestion nearly drove her to her knees. Whatever she expected, it wasn't this. Not from a man as passionate as Hunter, or even from the distant being he had become. "I thought that only happened in marriages of convenience," she said, and was surprised by the calm she managed.

"Isn't that what this is? A convenience."

"I suppose it is." Biting her lip, countering pain with pain, she concentrated on the cold light of the setting sun. Could this be the same sun that had shone on Marlee's garden, where, before his mother and friends, Hunter made his vows to her? Or on the glory-spangled days that followed? Where was the warming radiance that would forever recall the silk of his caress on her naked body and the magic of his kiss?

When had Hunter, who couldn't get his fill of her, become a stranger speaking of convenience? Her mind was a jumble. Question tumbled over question. Because she had to know, without turning, she asked, "Do you regret tying yourself to me so soon?"

"Tying myself? My God, Beth, is that what you think?"

"I . . ." She couldn't voice her fear.

In three strides, he was standing behind her. His hands hovered over her shoulders before falling to his side. He knew he must not touch her. If he did, he would never say what he should. "I regret nothing for my sake. Only for yours." His whisper was urgent, ragged. "This marriage wasn't only to deal with the news stories or the reporters or even Eric, for that matter. It was for *me*. I wanted you so much, I grabbed at any excuse to keep you."

Beth's hands flew to her lips, stifling her cry. Hunter wanted her. Beyond that, nothing mattered.

His laugh was mocking and humorless. "Would it sicken you to know that I'm almost grateful to that damn reporter? In a perverted way, he gave me a week when nothing mattered." With a resigned gesture, he stopped. Silence fell between them, broken only by a sharp rasping breath that signaled the rise of his anger. Almost brutally, he muttered, "Like a fool, I never let myself consider what I've done to you with this marriage."

"Done to me?" She spun from the window. "You make it sound as if you've done something terrible."

"I have, in marking you with the stigma of the breed's woman."

"If you mean to shock me with the name, you haven't. I've heard it before, remember?" Her unwavering gaze held his. "There's no stigma or ugliness in it. The ugliness is in the people who don't know you. Who don't understand."

"You don't understand. The day may come when you hate me for what I am." His hands came up and with a will of their own, curved about the slight swell of her abdomen. "Because of my carelessness, you could be carrying a child." His voice dropped to a snarl of contempt. "My child. Another breed."

The crack of her hand across his face was thunderous in the still of the room. "How dare you!" she spat out in fury. "How dare you speak of yourself in that tone. Or of me."

Hunter's head was thrown back by the force of her blow; his face was somber beneath the brightening mark of her fingers. He was shocked by her fury and stunned by the blow, but the violence that was a part of his heritage and his life lay dormant. He would cut off his hand before he would hurt her. That privilege, he thought bitterly, was reserved for his tongue.

Beth hardly noticed his stillness that for anyone else would mean danger. "You're a person, whatever the mix of your blood. You name is *Slade*, not breed! I'm *Slade's* woman." Her hand rested where his had been. "This is *Slade's* child. I'll teach him to be proud of his father's people. As I would of mine, if the misbegotten child of a wanderer—"

"What did you say?" Hunter's eyes were dark fires, his face was ashen beneath its ruddy tan.

"I said misbegotten." Every syllable of the word was ripped from her tongue through gritted teeth. "Have you forgotten that I'm a bastard? Does it bother you? Do you want to—"

Hunter's hands caught in her hair, refusing to release her when she tried to jerk free. "Be still!" he commanded. Then as she obeyed he pleaded, "Tell me! For God's sake, tell me what you meant."

"What do you want to hear, Hunter? A lie? The truth? What?"

"It can't be." He was too stunned to think. "I was careless, but it's too soon. You couldn't begin to know."

"I don't need time or tests to tell me what my body knows." She shook his hands aside. "Your child is here." Folding both arms over her body, she said fiercely, "He'll be proud of every drop of blood in his veins, and if he's half the man I thought his father, I'll ask for nothing more."

"Beth." Hunter's mind spun like a whirligig. His disparaging remarks, the mockingly bitter expression of his own hurts and disappointments were forgotten. He felt as if he'd been ripped in half. In a leap of primitive pride—in the woman he'd chosen for his own, for the child who might be—a part of him knew the exhilaration of the procreating male. The other felt already the gathering storm of anguish that would come when they must leave him. Struggling with the tightness in his throat, he tried again. "Beth."

"Shh." With a slanting finger, she sealed his lips. Sliding her arms about his neck, she rose on tiptoe, kissing his brow, each eye, each cheek and slowly, with lingering care, his mouth. "I'm Slade's woman, Hunter Slade's woman, for as long as he wants me. But for this—" she touched his cheek as if she would heal the hurt where she struck him "—I have just one regret."

Incredulous and bemused, he was aware of her tawny blush of health and the quiet, glowing serenity of her smile. She was an exquisitely beautiful woman. His woman, and she would fight the world for him. In a voice rough with the desire he meant to deny, he asked, "What would that regret be, tiger lady?"

"That my husband doesn't realize that I'm not going anywhere. Not to another room or another place, until he sends me away. And that I have an ache here—" she touched her lips, then her left breast "—and here."

"Here?" He kissed her lips. Because she was and always would be irresistible, because promises and fears and prejudices were no equal to her wishes, his kiss deepened. His head lifted, his caress found the fullness of her breasts. "And here?" He soothed with a touch the flesh that flowed like warm honey in his palm. At her sigh of pleasure, he swept her into his arms. As the last light faded from the mountains, he took her with him to his bed to offer succor for her regret.

Night spread a black cloak over the earth. Dawn was only an illusion in a star-studded sky. The land was hushed and empty. Beth was not alone in its darkness. Her eyes strayed from the window where she stood to Hunter.

He was a proud man who kept his own counsel and tended his own wounds. He lived in a land where many judged him cruelly. Yet he would never leave it. His love for these mountains was as much a part of him as the Cherokee and English blood that filled his veins. He was too much man to run from trouble.

He would contend with the future as he had the past. As he had with dyslexia so severe he could see no more than two letters at once, requiring his brilliant mind to learn and relearn and learn again in the never-resolved struggle to read.

He would withdraw time and again in his hurt, but she would be with him. Waiting for the hurt to pass.

She moved to the bed. Her touch was light as she brushed a lock of midnight hair from his face. Her fingertips lingered lovingly at his mouth before moving to her naked abdomen. *"We'll* be waiting," she said huskily, for she believed with an unshakable faith that his seed was here, nurtured by her body.

Someday, for that reason if for no other, he would listen and he would believe when she said, I love you.

"Someday," she promised, and slipped beneath the covers, accepting him with the love he never let her speak as he turned to her in sleep.

Dawn had come and gone when Beth opened the door to The Morning Glory Boutique. She had risen with the sun, showered, dressed, scrounged the keys to the Mercedes and kissed Hunter. Evading his drowsy embrace with a laughing promise of later, she drove herself down the mountain. To her surprise, she was not the first to arrive.

"Raven!"

"Good morning, Mrs. Slade." The greeting rolled off Raven's tongue in a teasing Scottish burr. "You're early for a woman newly returned from her honeymoon."

"Not as early as you."

"There were a few things I wanted to get done before you came in." With a gesture, she indicated a tangle of colorful scarves lying on a counter. "Obviously, I didn't succeed."

"You've sacrificed more than a week of your time. You didn't have to come in today."

"Of course, I didn't. I wanted to." A smile lighted Raven's serene face. "It's your first day home. There could be many calls on your time. In the shop and out."

"You're here in case the operative word is *out.*"

"That was my intention."

"I've imposed enough on a brand-new friendship."

"Is that how you measure your friendships, Beth?" Raven asked. "By time?"

Beth picked up a scarf from the colorful profusion, sliding it through her fingers like liquid amber. "I don't know how I measure friendships. Friends were never a part of my life."

"Until now, when you have so many."

"That's as frightening as it is wonderful."

"It needn't be. Your instincts are good. Trust them."

"Sometimes I wonder how one so young could be so wise."

"Not so young." Raven's shrug was eloquent, as she was in everything. "And regrettably, not always so wise."

"I could argue both points, but I won't. Right now, my instincts are saying I should get to work to make up for lost time and to let nothing interrupt me."

"Nothing?"

"Absolutely!" Beth lifted the gauzy scarf and studied its delicate weave before the light. "This is a stunning piece of workmanship. Where did it come from?"

Raven chuckled in an undertone.

"Did I say something funny?"

"I was wondering whose instinct would be stronger. Yours—" Raven nodded to the door "—or his."

"What?" Beth whirled, and Hunter was there by the door. An incongruously dainty basket hung from one arm, and his dark, glittering gaze was solely for her.

"Good morning," he said as the bell over the opening door jangled.

"Good morning." Beth felt a flush rising in her cheeks at the hunger in his gaze.

"You left without saying a proper goodbye."

"You were sleepy."

"I wouldn't have been for long."

"I needed to get to the shop."

"You would have. Eventually." His gaze turned to Raven. "Morning, Raven."

"Morning, Hunter."

"You're going to be here awhile?"

"Certainly."

"Then you won't mind if I kidnap Beth."

"Not at all."

"Wait a minute," Beth said, interrupting their tongue-in-cheek banter. "Don't I have something to say about this?"

"No," Hunter and Raven said in unison.

"Beth, my dear." Raven took the scarf from her friend's hand. "You're outnumbered and outsized, and I don't think I'd argue with the look in the man's eye."

"But . . ."

"I've handled the shop for over a week. I can for one more day."

"I give up. I'm surrounded." Beth threw up her hands in defeat. She was laughing as she linked her arm through Hunter's and let him lead her to the street. "Just where is it I'm being taken?"

"In the poetic language of the mountains—to a place where water tumbles from the mountain into a lake that flows deep and still. Where the meadow lies green and wildflowers bloom."

"Morning glories?"

Hunter nodded. He looked down at her, at her shining face. In this moment she was the child she'd never been. Unspoiled, unjaded, finding pleasure in the simplest things. Her enthusiasm was contagious and he found himself looking at his world with fresh eyes, finding beauty where there had been none. "It won't be coffee at dawn as I intended. We'll save that for next time."

"It sounds like the loveliest place."

"It will be," Hunter promised, "when you're there."

The meadow was an improbable cul-de-sac nestled in the shadow of a jagged peak. A waterfall that began as a cataract at the precipice roared down the sheer rock face in an avalanche of white water. A great outcropping of granite jutting from the escarpment slowed its pace, cleaving through the torrent, tearing it asunder. From the misty spray created by the collision of tons of water with tons of granite, what had been one emerged as two.

The greater, with a mighty leap, regathered its force and plummeted down once more like a silver juggernaut. The second, a tiny fragment diverted from the smooth rock wall, found its own placid path. Flowing from stone to stone in countless cascades, it tumbled down the mountainside, spilling at last into the lake by the meadow. Hunter sat on a Cherokee mat, the forgotten picnic basket at his feet, watching as Beth explored. The roar of the cataract, which should have deafened, wrapped them in an utter quiet, sealing them in a private world where each muted sound was a perfect harmony for her laughter.

Beth looked up from a trailing bouquet of morning glories. "It is lovely."

Hunter smiled but did not answer for she had already turned to gather another blossom from the gnarled and stunted trunk of an evergreen. He watched as she knelt over a flower that reflected the pale pink flush of her cheeks, and another as blue as her eyes when they darkened in passion. The meadow produced an abundance of trumpetlike blossoms. Before Beth, Hunter had seen only a weed, a mongrel like himself.

He pushed the thought away. He wouldn't spoil this stolen moment with gloom. The threat of Eric Weston, the cloud of prejudice and even concern for the child Beth might be carrying could keep for another time. This day was Beth's. One more than he'd hoped to have with her.

Beth laughed again. The sound drifted through the misty morning air. It was a golden day, and nothing could tarnish it.

She beckoned him to her at the water's edge. One by one, she tossed the delicate flowers into the lake. In the mirrored surface, the reflected mountain was bedecked with a garland of color. "I thought I understood your love of this land and how it kept you here, but I didn't. Not until now."

"Neither did I. Not completely," Hunter said with a catch in his voice. "Until I saw it through your eyes."

Beth drew his hand to her cheek. It was September, the morning glories were blooming and she was still here. Still with Hunter. "Thank you."

"For what?"

"For more than you can ever know, but especially for this day. There's one more thing I'd like to do."

"And that is?" Whatever it was, he would move heaven and earth to give it to her.

"I want to swim in the lake with the morning glories. I want to feel every part of this day, to make it truly mine."

Hunter was not surprised. In the halcyon days of their honeymoon, he discovered that she loved the water and was an amazing, perhaps even a talented swimmer. Though they never discussed it, he suspected it was the one pleasure she was allowed as a child. After all, he thought in rising anger toward a mother he liked less and less with each discovery, water had no sharp edges that could mar the perfection of the marketable product.

No anger, not even of the righteous sort, could survive the shining blue gaze. Her heart was in her eyes and Hunter's melted. Softly, because words were almost beyond him, he cautioned, "The lake will be cold."

"I know, but you can warm me."

"My pleasure, Mrs. Slade."

She stepped a single step away. Her eyes never left his as, piece by piece, her clothing was discarded. First her blouse, a concoction of no-nonsense cotton. Then her bra, a totally delicious nonsensical wisp of lace that hugged her breasts, revealing only slightly less than when it floated to the ground. Without hesitation, the slim black skirt followed. After that, slowly, with teasing care, the sheer, black stockings. Beth was reveling in a newfound confidence, an uninhibited sexuality.

With her last garment gone, she stood before him unselfconsciously, as if a mountain meadow was the most natural place in the world for a woman to stand naked before her lover. Rising on tiptoe, her breasts and thighs burning his skin, she kissed him. Her lips lingered, speaking of other wishes, other needs.

"I won't be long," she promised.

Beth swam in the crystal water. Like a fairy creature, she weaved among the floating flowers. Diving beneath the surface, she turned and glided. As if the water were Hunter's hand, she arched and moved in erotic delight. And in the wind that stirred the treetops, Hunter heard the echo of music.

When she was through swimming, he was waiting to dry her. He had no towel, but his shirt sufficed. After the last droplet was tenderly and unhurriedly banished, he took her in his arms, and walked to the mat. In the bright, glittering haze of the meadow, with their bodies twining like morning glories, he warmed her.

* * *

Christen peered over the tiny glasses perched on her nose. She sat behind the desk of the communal office she shared with Zachary and Nathan. Beth was her last patient for the day. "Marriage to Hunter agrees with you."

"Is it that obvious?" Beth asked around a smile.

"Let's just say I don't think you could hide it. Not at the moment." She laid the report she had been reading on her desk. "Most especially not in the months to come."

"When my pregnancy begins to show."

Christen tossed the reading glasses aside. "This blood test shows that you were right. You are pregnant. Barely."

Beth laughed. In the three days since the morning at the meadow, she'd laughed a lot. "How can one be barely pregnant?"

It was Christen's turn to laugh. "When some of the more obvious changes begin to take place, you'll know. You don't seem the type for morning sickness, but you can expect some tenderness in your breasts, and you might find that you need more sleep. Now that the rest of us can be as sure as you were, we'll do a complete examination or, if you'd like, I can refer you to an obstetrician."

"I'd rather you and Zachary and Nathan were with us during this pregnancy. It would mean a great deal to Hunter if his best friends brought his child into the world. It's not that uncommon, is it, for the women of the valley to choose to have their babies here in the clinic? As you did with Greg."

"It would mean a great deal to us, too. But only if your term is uneventful, with no complications."

"You don't anticipate any problems!"

"You're an exceptionally healthy woman and you should have a healthy baby." Christen leaned back in her chair, folding her hands beneath her chin thoughtfully. "You really want this baby, don't you?"

"More than I realized. I've wanted a baby for a long time, but this is special."

"Because the child is Hunter's."

"Yes."

"How does he feel?"

"I'm sure you can guess." Beth looked down at her hands folded protectively over her abdomen. She did not want Christen to see her sudden uncertainty. "He's happy, but he's worried about me, and he's afraid this child will have to deal with the cruelties and prejudices that almost destroyed his life."

"Barring the unforeseen, you should be fine, and times have changed since Hunter and I were children. Prejudice exists, but it isn't so rampant. Go home. Tell him tonight over dinner by candlelight that you're going to have a very healthy baby and that together, you can fight any battle. When the woman he loves is pregnant, even the bravest man can be frightened. Reassure him. Tell him you love him." Christen chuckled with some gleeful secret. "It works," she said almost to herself. "Every time."

Beth stood, ducking her head to hide her faltering smile. She couldn't tell Christen that her last advice was impossible. She loved Hunter beyond any doubt. In her heart, she had to believe this baby was an expression of his love. Yet the simple phrase that would mean so much had never been spoken between them. Hunter was a tender and passionate lover. In their moments together, he whispered beautiful things, but never the most beautiful of all. Never, I love you. And, with some sixth sense, he knew when she ached to say them, and in one way or another, he prevented it.

Christen snapped her fingers to recall Beth's attention. "Planning your celebration already?"

"What?"

"Never mind." Drawing a prescription pad from the pocket of her lab coat, she tore the top sheet off and handed it to Beth. "On your way home, stop by the pharmacy and get this filled. It's a simple vitamin and a little calcium that I'd like you to take. If you have no problems, come back in three weeks."

"That's it?"

"That's it. Now scoot. And remember, tell him you love him. That fixes everything."

"I will," Beth promised, and managed a smile as she added in her heart, someday.

Ten

"**H**ow would you feel about playing hooky?"

Beth turned in the passenger's seat of the Mercedes with a questioning look for Hunter. "What do you have in mind?"

"There's no law that says you have to reopen the boutique this afternoon. We can forget that Christmas is only two weeks away and that you're busier than the dickens. We could just keep driving, maybe stop in at Bert's for a piece of pie."

"Pie! After one of Bell's lunches? Are you kidding?"

"You ate like a bird."

She put down the book she had been scanning. "I didn't eat everything in sight, as you thought I should, but I ate sensibly. I'm not a lumberjack."

Hunter refused to be diverted. "But you are pregnant and you're not as big as most ladies are. I mean, some of them are…'' Searching for a word but failing, he shrugged and said, ''Well, they're pretty big, and you're just—''

''Well rounded?'' Beth supplied. ''Actually, I'm huge for the end of the first trimester.'' She laughed, delighted with her swollen belly. ''For me, it's been instant pregnancy. Christen says I'm healthy, and considering the size of the baby's father, there's nothing to be alarmed about.''

''You're sure?''

''I have every faith in her judgment. I'm fine, Hunter. If I weren't, I'd tell you. You don't have to watch every move I make in the next six months.''

''I'm not.''

''Then prove it. Go to your studio. Work! I'm sure you have something you want to get back to.''

Hunter couldn't deny that something had caught his imagination and fired his enthusiasm.

''Go!'' She made a sweeping gesture with her hands. ''After a two-hour lunch at Nathan's, I've been hovered over enough. Anyway, I have an appointment with Raven in fifteen minutes.''

''You win.'' Hunter made a right turn, then pulled to the curb before the boutique. Daring her to leave the car, he came around, opened her door and offered his hand. When she was standing on the street, he gathered the lapels of her coat tighter about her neck. ''I'm going. First to the bank, then the studio.'' Drawing her to him, he nuzzled her cheek. ''But I'll be back.''

''Oh yeah?''

''Count on it.'' He kissed her quickly and was gone.

As he drove away, leaving her alone in the cold of a December day, a secret worry nagged at her. He made her feel she and his child were the most precious part of his life. Yet he held himself aloof. The barriers he'd needed to survive were less visible, but still there, keeping safe a part he would not let her touch. Hunter's cornerstone, kept for years inviolate, to rebuild upon when all else was gone.

Thoughtfully, she turned the key in the lock and flipped the Out To Lunch sign over as she closed the door. The shop was Hunter's creation as much as her own. He believed in her. The rich display before her was proof. But not in her heart. "I love you, Hunter. I'd never hurt you. Why won't you listen and believe?" she whispered softly. "You love me. I feel it here." Her hands rested on the swell of his child. "Beyond that, what could matter?"

A fickle wind rose suddenly, moaning its sad song about the roof. Windows chattered and walls creaked. Beth shivered in imagined cold and discovered that she was tired after all. Shrugging out of her coat, she crossed to a collection of rare books. The book she'd taken with her from Hunter's car, discovered by Bell at an auction, would be a fine addition.

From her private collection, she selected one of a growing library on dyslexia. Settled at a table by the window, she read, waiting for Raven.

"Raven!" Beth laid her book aside and rose to meet her friend. "It's so good to see you. It's been months."

Raven embraced Beth and stepped away. "Months of growing, I'd say." Her blue-gray eyes twinkled as she admired Beth's altered body.

Beth only shrugged, her delight in herself overshadowed by her worries of Hunter. "Where are your twin shadows?" she asked, referring to the dogs that were Raven's constant companions.

"Dropped them off at the vet on my way up the mountain."

"Are they ill?"

"Routine checkup."

Beth led Raven to the table. "If the afternoon continues as it has been, we can talk uninterrupted. The threat of rain has driven away all my customers."

Taking the seat Beth offered, Raven studied her critically. "How are you? Really."

"I'm fine."

"And the babe?"

"Just as fine."

"I was hoping you'd say better. Something's bothering you."

Beth released Raven's hands. "You're very perceptive."

"And you don't want to talk about it."

"It's just a little misunderstanding that only Hunter and I can resolve."

"A quarrel?"

"I wish it were that simple. It's nothing new. Sometimes it gets me down."

"As it has today," Raven said gently. "I'll wait for a better time to show you the pieces I brought."

"No! Your work is exactly what I need today."

"There's not that much, but it's something new. I hope you'll like it."

The threat of rain worsened; the quiet afternoon continued. Beth and Raven were deep in discussion of an exquisite vessel more like lacy turquoise than clay when the bell over the door jangled.

Beth turned to greet her customer. Her gasp was a strangled scream. Her smile froze. The fragile azure bowl nearly slipped from her fingers before she set it aside with exaggerated care.

"Eric." His name was a trembling breath as she struggled for control. Her world, imperfect, troubled, but still wonderful, was crashing at her feet.

"I see you haven't forgotten me." The sleek, blond man, with his impeccable clothes and his perfect smile, stepped farther into the shop.

She had forgotten, Beth realized. Impossible as it seemed, though he was the reason for her marriage to Hunter, she had put Eric Weston from her mind. It had been months since she had looked over her shoulder.

"You look surprised, Elizabeth. Surely you knew I would come. By the way, my dear, the picture in that sleazy, yellow journal was atrocious. The savage and his woman, indeed!" He turned his handsome head, taking in every aspect of the shop. His gaze settled on silent Raven, then arrogantly dismissed her.

"I knew you'd see it, somehow, but I hoped you'd given up," Beth said in a strained voice.

"Because of this farce of a marriage legitimizing a sordid little affair? Don't be ridiculous." His laugh was unperturbed. "I waited a few months to let you get this man out of your system. Now I've come to take you home with me, where you belong."

"This is my home, Eric."

"Elizabeth, darling, your home is with me. You're mine. You always have been. You always will be. I've let you have your fling, your little independence. Now it's over." He was scolding his wayward child. "You knew I would come for you just as I always have. How many times have you hidden, forcing me to have to find you, only to have you run away again? This time, you've been especially naughty. I think I have to teach you a lesson."

Raven looked from Beth to Eric. Her stare was stony gray, her expression wooden. Rising slowly, she murmured something unintelligible about privacy and left them. Beth wanted desperately to call her back, but didn't. Like a fool, she'd involved too many innocent people in the ugliness of her life.

Eric's gaze followed Raven until the door of the private office shut her from view. His face altered. He was as handsome, but beneath the unflawed features, Beth saw vicious anger. The anger was not reflected in his voice. As if nothing had changed, he said conversationally, "If divorce didn't stop me, did you think some backwoods marriage would?"

"I'm not your possession, Eric. I never was."

"You're mistaken. You were bought and paid for. There was precious little difference between you and a whore, was there?"

Beth's hands flew to her face, stifling her cry.

Eric smiled. "The truth hurts, does it?"

It did. Not because he said it, but because it was so nearly what she thought of herself. *Had* thought of herself, she corrected. No more. Not since Hunter.

Eric mesmerized and repulsed her. He was using shame to cripple her, but with Hunter, there was no shame. Beth found her courage. Her head came up. "I'm not a whore. If I was ever for sale, I'm not anymore."

"No?" He quirked an eyebrow, his smile was smug.

"No. I'm not going to run from you ever again. There's more at stake than myself or even Hunter."

He was moving closer, a snake charming a bird. "A backwoodsman in a backwater town? Don't be ridiculous. You're more suited to the life I can give you. You wanted it before, you will again, once I take you back to the casinos and the parties."

"You were my mother's dream. She's dead now and I don't have to pretend anymore. I never wanted anything from you."

He clicked his tongue. "Don't pout, my sweet. You'll get over the little dancer. She was just a diversion."

"Little dancer?" For a moment, Beth was puzzled, then she threw back her head in genuine laughter. "You think

I'm upset about some dancer? Dear heaven, Eric! I didn't even know."

"Of course, you did, Elizabeth. This is just your silly little way of getting even. An affair for an affair."

"You're mad, Eric. Totally, completely, certifiably insane."

"Bitch!" With a stride, he was towering over her. The smooth, unctuous smile supplanted by rage, indeed, akin to dementia. "Nobody calls me crazy. Do you hear me?" His hand was raised to strike her. His hands closed into bludgeoning fists. His voice rose to an unrecognizable shriek. "Nobody!"

"Touch her, Weston, and I'll kill you." Hunter's voice was beautiful, deadly.

Eric's hand jerked open in surprise. His fingers stabbed the air impotently.

In that moment, Eric ceased to exist. For Beth, there was only the man who stood in the doorway. She had heard that quiet voice before, coaxing a callow fool to destruction. Now, perhaps, paving the way to his own. "No!" Beth rose on shaking legs, concerned for nothing but the man she loved. "Hunter." Her voice fell to a ragged whisper. "Please, no!"

"Ahh, the backwoodsman to the rescue." Eric spun like a ballet dancer toward the door. His eyes widened at the fierce visage of the huge man he'd thought to intimidate with his sarcasm. "My dear," he said to Beth, "was the Journal right? Do I detect a bit of the blanket in your lover?"

"Damn you, Eric," Beth snapped, angered at the denigrating reference to Hunter's Indian Heritage. "If you have a brain in your head, you'll shut your mouth and leave."

"Not yet, Beth," Hunter said. "Weston and I have something to settle."

"Hunter, please," she pleaded.

"I won't hurt him, I promise," Hunter said, and added softly, "not unless he makes me."

"Why, Elizabeth," Eric drawled, "worried about me after all?"

"No, Weston," Hunter answered for her. "She's worried about me and what it would do to my life if I have to kill you."

Hunter's calm observation was more chilling than a threat. Eric's confidence shriveled. "Elizabeth is mine," he said petulantly. "Mine."

"The woman who was Elizabeth Weston might have belonged to you." Hunter advanced. Eric retreated, his bravado faltering. "That woman ceased to exist the day her mother died. She's Beth Slade now."

"A squaw!" Eric spat out the words, struggling to gain control.

"She's been called that before. I don't think it bothered her," Hunter said mildly. Keeping careful watch on Eric, he stretched his hand to her. "Beth."

"I'm here." Taking his hand, she stepped to Hunter's side.

With his first full glimpse of her body, Eric's eyes widened in horror. "My God! You're breeding! It's bad enough that you let this…person put his hands on you. Now this."

Refusing to acknowledge his slur, Beth tried to reason with him. "There was never anything between us but an empty marriage, Eric. It ended long ago. My life is with Hunter now, and with his child. Accept it. Quit torturing yourself and me. Put me out of your mind and get on with your life."

Eric's laugh was ugly. "I'll put you out of my life, all right. I could forgive your letting another man put his hands on you." He was working himself into a maddened frenzy. His gesture toward Beth's gently swollen body was filled with contempt. "A brat is too much."

"Then you know there's nothing here for you," Hunter said. "There never was. Do as Beth asked. Leave. Now."

Eric's malevolent gaze moved from Hunter to Beth. In the eerie silence that fell over them, he stared at her. His mouth worked, his unspoken curses as vitriolic as those spoken. At last, he bared his teeth in a parody of a smile that left his eyes cold. "Yes." The word was the hiss of a snake ready to strike.

Hunter tensed. The quiet was a terrible, writhing thing. He waited.

Eric laughed. The sound of it echoed off the ceiling and the walls. "Ah, yes." He turned away. He was a jerky stick figure, the sly grace gone, as he walked to the front of the shop. With his hand on the door, he fired a parting shot. "You're welcome to her, Slade. The woman I knew is dead."

Hunter drew Beth to him. "No, Weston. The woman you knew never existed at all."

The door slammed after Eric, and Beth slumped against Hunter. "It's over," she whispered. "Really over."

"Over," Hunter said in a flat voice.

"How did you know?" She looked up at him from the sanctuary of his arms. "I needed you and you came."

"Raven saw me at the bank earlier. She gambled that I was still there."

"Raven," Beth called out to her friend.

The dark-haired woman stepped from the office, an ornately carved cane in her hand. "Did you think I would desert you?"

"Were you planning to use that?" Hunter asked.

"If need be." Raven's calm reply left no doubt of her violent intent.

Beth's laugh was shrill, rising in a note of hysteria cut short by her hand clamped over her mouth. Leaving Hunter, she hugged Raven fiercely. "What would I do without you? All of you?"

Raven returned her embrace. "You would've done no less."

"Could I ask one more thing of you?" Hunter's voice was an anxious rumble as he addressed Raven.

"You don't have to ask." She met his gaze levelly, understanding what he wanted and why. Beth was pregnant. She'd had a shock. Hunter's first stop would be the clinic and then home, where she could rest and recover. "I'll close up. Be careful, the storm will be here soon. Just let me know what the doctor says."

"I will." As if she would break, Hunter led Beth away.

Hunter watched as Beth lay sleeping. Her hair rippled over the pillow. Her lashes were a fine, gold mist on her cheeks. Her mouth curled in a peaceful smile. In the week since Eric had walked out of her life for good, her smile remained constant. Each day, she was like a flower opening to the sun. When Hunter looked at her, he saw a beautiful dream.

"An impossible dream." He turned to the window. Dawn was breaking. Today, not even the land he loved, washed clean by a week of rain and bathed in crimson by the rising sun, could ease his regret. Remembering how she had come to him in the night, he whispered, "Dear, God! How can I let her go?"

"Hunter?"

Her drowsy voice wrapped around him like a caress. He stiffened. Hurting. Determined. He could let her go. He would be cutting his heart out, but he must. For her sake, for the child. He was suddenly cold despite the banked embers glowing in the open fireplace. When Beth went, taking the sun from his life, he would never be warm again.

"Have you been awake long?" she asked.

He turned, steeling himself against the desire that would sweep over him. Her skin was dewy from her sleep, her eyes languid with remembered passion. Disheveled tendrils of gleaming gold framed her face. Her lips invited his kiss. He could no more deny the rise of his passion than he could the tides of the sea. But he could silence his heart and speak with the voice of reason. "Beth."

Her name rang hollowly, like a black omen in the bright morning stillness. The blush of her cheeks faded. The languid look in her eyes was replaced by the dread he hated. Her smile vanished. Clutching the sheet to her naked breasts, she rose to an upright position. She watched him, eyes fearful in a pallid face.

"We have to talk." He waited for a response, but there was none. He sensed that despite her bright cheeriness of the past week, she had expected this moment and knew what he meant to say. "I've thought about this day for a long time. The day when we would decide it was time for you to leave."

He paced the floor. He couldn't look at her and keep his wits about him. "This marriage was for a purpose. When Eric Weston stepped out of your life for good, that purpose was done. There's nothing to keep you here now. We can find a buyer for the boutique, or perhaps someone to run it. I've spoken to Marlee. She'd be delighted if you'd live with her until the baby comes. After that, you can decide what you want to do with your life. Money will never be a problem."

He stopped by the window. A drop of moisture trickled down the frosted pane, the tear he could not shed. Not yet. He wore only the trousers he had pulled on when he discovered sleep was impossible. Now he slid his hands into the pockets to hide their trembling. Beth had been tied to cripples all her life—her mother, Eric. He wouldn't add himself to the list.

As if in confirmation, a voice from the past, mute these many months, found its tongue. *No intelligent woman in her right mind could love a backwoods half-breed...*

Hunter shuddered, sickened by the cruel honesty of that voice. "I want you to find a better life than I can give you. For yourself and for my child."

In the sepulchral hush, Hunter felt alone, as if Beth had already gone from him. "You have so much to give to the child and to a man you can love. Your life is waiting somewhere out there. You told Eric to get on with his life. So should you."

Beth bowed her head to hide her face. She'd prayed this day would never come. Hunter loved her; she had to believe he did for the sake of her child. But not enough. She never wanted to be Eric's possession, but she would settle for any crumb from Hunter. There was one chance and she was not too proud to try. "Do you truly want another man to raise your son?"

Without benefit of any test, Beth was as certain she carried a male child as she had been of his conception. Hunter did not doubt her. "I could never read to him, Beth."

A simple sentence, filled with years of hurt and frustration, of the shame he would spare his child. Beth longed to go to him and comfort him, but she dared not. "You haven't answered my question. Look at me," she commanded. "Look at me and tell me you want another man to sleep with me, to hold me and make love to me and call your son his."

He couldn't look at her. For the first time in his life Hunter chose the cowardly way. His back was still turned when he whispered, "I want what's best for both of you. That isn't me."

"All right," Beth said quietly. She had her answer. Not the one Hunter thought he'd given. What was best for her

was Hunter. That was her answer, but for now, she woul
do as he asked. "I'll begin making my plans today."

"Christmas is a week away. Will you wait till then?"

"No. Why prolong it any more than we have to?"

Hunter drew a long, painful breath. His shoulder
slumped. "Will you let me drive you to the boutique?"

"If you wish. I need to be there early for an appointmen
with Raven. I'd like to be alone for a while now."

He turned then, his eyes lingering long on the nakednes
she made no effort to hide. "I'll dress at the studio and wa
for you."

When he was gone, Beth left their bed. At the window
where he had stood, with only the memory of his caresses t
clothe her, she watched an ever-changing dawn. She ha
come to the mountains seeking a hiding place and had dis
covered a land of majesty and love. She wouldn't lose ei
ther so easily. She would keep silent and make her ow
plans.

"It has to work." She stroked the swell of her abdomen
"Your father is a proud, stubborn man. He's overcome im
possible odds. What's a little thing like reading when h
works magic with his hands? No argument will change hi
mind. So we'll make our case by doing exactly as he asked
We'll go. We'll leave the mountain. But I promise you," sh
said fervently, "your first breath will be drawn here."

Closing her eyes, she breathed a silent prayer. Dear God
she had to be right. By going, she had to make Hunter re
alize he couldn't live without her any more than she coul
live without him. "He must!" she said, trying to quiet he
doubts with the sound of her voice. When she could not, sh
faced them squarely. She hadn't been very wise in the past
or strong enough to fight for what she wanted and be
lieved. This time she would be. If she was wrong, a part o
her would die, but she would survive. She had a reason t
survive.

"I will have his son."

"Are you ready?" At her nod, Hunter started to take her arm, then decided it was best not to touch her. Bitterly, he realized he alone had turned lovers into strangers.

"I can drive myself." Beth was pale and too calm.

"The river's at flood stage. I don't want you driving over the bridge at the base of the mountain." He expected an argument but got none. Beth's unquestioning acceptance was unsettling. What did he want? Tears, anger? Would he feel less like a heel if she punished him? Tough luck, Slade, he snarled at himself. The lady's too classy for revenge. His wounds would remain self-inflicted.

In the Range Rover, called back into service for the rain, Hunter left her to her thoughts. He'd said more than enough for her lifetime. He turned his attention to the road. The incline was not treacherous, but required care in negotiating its muddy twists and turns. They were down and almost across the ancient wooden bridge when he let himself relax. He had looked away from the road, at Beth, simply because he needed the sight of her, when he knew something was dreadfully wrong.

First, it was the sound. A deep, mournful groan of shifting wood, followed immediately by the shriek of straining metal. Within a millisecond, before Hunter could cry out a warning or Beth could scream, a beam popped like a toothpick. The bridge leaned, shuddered once and collapsed, taking the Range Rover with it into the flooding river.

The muddy water was swift and frigid. The Range Rover lay submerged on its side, blocking Beth's escape. In the midst of the furor that sent them tumbling into the river, Hunter had heard one sound. Beth's indrawn breath. As he struggled to open his door against the pressure of the river, he was thankful for the seconds that breath would give him. His own lungs were screaming from his efforts when he

reached for her through the murky water. Beth was already
rising from the seat and twisting past the steering wheel to
meet him.

Hunter caught her about the waist. As he fought the current, he saw her strength was nearly gone, sapped by shock
and cold. "Can you lock your arms about my neck?" At her
nod, he whispered, "Good girl. Now, honey, hold on to me.
No matter what."

He let the current take them downstream, struggling,
fighting, working his way toward the shore. When he could
touch bottom, he waded through the churning debris with
Beth in his arms. His shirt was torn, his body battered and
bruised by the time he lifted her wearily to an overhanging
limb. "The banks of the river are too steep here to climb.
Can you hold on while I go downstream . . . ?"

"Hunter!" Beth's scream came too late. A massive beam,
torn from the fallen bridge by the flood, bore down on him.
With the power of the river behind it, it pounded into him,
undercutting his legs, throwing him with a skull-cracking
force against the branch where Beth sat. His body went slack
and the hungry water swallowed him.

Beth plunged into the water, exhaustion forgotten. The
part of her mind that was functioning knew she had only
seconds before he would be swept away. She did not feel the
smaller debris from the bridge pummeling her body as she
made one desperate lunge for him, and then another. She
was losing him. Then miraculously, she pulled him from a
tangle of flotsam. She tried to lift him from the water but
couldn't. It took all she had to keep the greedy river from
snatching him from her.

No! You can't have him!

The silent cry dragged the last bit of strength from the
bottom of her reserve. Like a harridan, she shrieked and
cursed and drove herself on, dragging him with her to the

riverbank. Catching a root at the water's edge, she clung there, hurt, spent, but keeping his head above the current.

Plastered with mud, with rubbish catching in her hair, she held him. He groaned once, then was silent. His body was deadweight as she fought the water that wanted him.

The day grew brighter. Time crawled by. Beth's legs were numb from the cold. Her shoulders felt as if her arms had been ripped from their sockets. Her body was a mass of dull aches.

An ache in her back turned ugly. Her body convulsed, caught in the vice of a powerful contraction. She swayed and stumbled, the brute force of pain drove her to her knees. Water closed over her head, mud filled her mouth and nose. Sputtering and gasping for breath, she struggled to her feet. Rigid from the pain, she gathered Hunter closer and clung to him. The cramp passed, dwindling gradually away, and there was hope. Five minutes later, that hope was destroyed. A second contraction seized her, this one more vicious than the first.

"Please! No!" she cried out. "Please, not my baby." Then she was silent.

Contraction followed contraction. Beth lost track of the number as she battled for Hunter. Mercifully, when reality became too much to bear, her mind slipped into delirium. When Zachary's voice said gently, "It's all right, Beth, you can let him go, I have him," she thought it was a dream. Then strong arms were taking her precious burden while others were lifting her from the water.

She heard disjointed phrases, of Raven, a missed appointment, worry. A call to Hunter's friends, a search, the bridge. Then...

"My God!" The voice was Christen's. "She's bleeding." Then crisply, the no-nonsense professional. "Miscarriage. Get her to the clinic."

"Hunter!" Beth cried as a needle pricked her arm and sh
slid into oblivion.

Beth. Hunter's voice called to her. She opened her eye
She was alone. Sunlight streamed through a window
warming her face with its light. For a moment, she was di
oriented, then she remembered vague voices explaining wha
she cried out to know.

The bridge. Eric. Sabotage. Her baby.

Torn fingers crept over the sheet to her body. Flat. Lif
less. Barren.

Her heartache began then, bringing with it the remem
brance of another grief. Hunter's. The sound of it whi
pered in her memory, his low, ragged voice pleading with he
to live.

Her baby was dead, but Hunter was alive. She had trade
one for the other. "Hunter is alive!"

"Yes." A cool hand stroked her forehead. Bell had rise
from her seat beyond Beth's vision. "My son is alive b
cause of you."

"Where is he?"

"He left when we moved you from the clinic to N
than's. When he knew you were out of danger."

"Oh, God! He's gone after Eric."

"He felt he must."

"But we can't be sure Eric caused the bridge to co
lapse."

"There were witnesses. Not of the sabotage, but of h
purchases. The equipment he needed to undermine the met
braces. The flood water did the rest."

"Hunter mustn't... Eric's not worth this. Neither am I."

"Shh. Be calm," Bell crooned. "Hunter will do nothi
foolish. He finally realizes he has too much to lose. Re
now. Sleep. It will pass the time until he returns."

In the evening of the second day, Beth woke to find Raven sitting by her bedside. She stretched out her hand to her friend. "I owe you my thanks for sending up the alarm when I missed our appointment."

Raven shrugged with her charming eloquence. "If you don't mind, I won't say it was my pleasure."

"I won't mind." Beth's hand returned to her abdomen. She fell silent.

"I'm sorry about the baby," Raven said quietly. "Nothing can change that, but perhaps these will cheer you a bit." Setting a basket of flowers and a small package on the bed, she backed away. "Before you say any more, I was instructed to deliver them and leave you alone." Remembering the weary man who had called from the hunt asking this one favor, she kissed Beth's forehead and left her.

With unsteady hands, Beth lifted the package from the swirl of white sheet. When the pale yellow ribbon was discarded and the lid set aside, nestled inside in a profusion of tissue was a tiny replica of Beth kneeling in a bed of morning glories, looking as she would have looked in the full bloom of pregnancy. Hunter called it simply *Glory*.

In the perfectly sculpted figure was all the love Hunter had never spoken. Placing the figure on the bedside table where she had only to turn her head to see it, she took the note from the tiny bouquet of yellow roses. Drawing the card from its envelope with shimmering eyes, she read the words she had never heard, written in a rough hand she had never seen.

Hunter had written simply, "I love you."

"Yes," Beth whispered, and the first smile in many days tilted the corners of her mouth.

Epilogue

"Hello, tiger lady." Hunter waited in the twilight fo[r] Beth's eyes to open. The search though the mountain wil[der]derness was done and he had come directly to her. He wa[s] weary, dirty and bruised, but none of it would matter if sh[e] smiled at him.

"Hunter." Her smile. Slow, drowsy, tender. "You'r[e] home!"

"I couldn't stay away any longer."

"Eric?" He heard her fear. Not for Eric Weston or her[self]. self. For the breed, the fool who lost a precious part o[f] himself in a mountain stream. For Hunter Slade. For he[r] love.

He looked down into her face, thin and wan from her or[deal]. deal. A band of steel closed about his throat; the ache o[f] tears never shed in a lifetime of hurting. Beth frowned at hi[s] silence, her deep anxious breath drew him from his inertia.

"Don't fret, love." He stroked the lines from her fore-head. "I didn't harm him. I never intended to. He took care of it himself. The sheriff's trackers cornered him at the edge of a ravine. The man was truly mad. He took a crazy chance." Hunter's hand grew still. "Eric fell, Beth. He's alive, but barely. He'll never be a threat again."

"Why, Hunter?"

"Why didn't I beat him to a pulp with my bare hands like I wanted to?" He took her hurt hand in his, bowing to kiss each torn nail. "The price of revenge was far too dear if, in the end, it took me from you."

Beth's eyelashes dipped to her cheeks, but not before he saw the glitter of happiness. He had given her the answer she wanted. Hunter wondered at this splendid woman, who accepted him as he was, who never fought more gallantly than when she fought for him. His tiger lady, who loved him so completely that his life meant more than her own. More than the life of their unborn child.

"Sweetheart, I'm sorry. So sorry." Forgetting his dusty clothing and the roughness of a two-day growth of beard, he curled on the pristine sheet beside her. Taking her in his arms, meaning to hold her, he discovered it was he who was held. He who was comforted in her arms. The healing tears were his, dried by her soft kisses.

"I didn't know that love is total commitment. That it's sacrifice—" His voice broke. He lay for a time with his arm over his eyes, his body rigid. When the storm of emotion passed, he said softly, "Because I didn't know, I wouldn't believe. I nearly let the past cheat us of the future. Now, I've learned. Like revenge, the cost of my lesson was too dear." Rising on one elbow, with the length of his body pressed to hers, he stroked her face. "Your love is the gift of my life. Can it survive the sacrifice of our child?"

"Don't," Beth pleaded. Cupping her hand about his battered face, she gazed into his tortured eyes. "I did what

I had to do. There was no time for choices. I'll grieve fo him and wonder what he might have been, but if that mo ment could be reduced to choices, my choice would be th same. I love you, Hunter.''

He gathered her to him. ''How did a breed who can' carve a sign unless his mother writes out the words get woman like you?''

He spoke completely without rancor. In the aftermath o tragedy, he had moved one more step beyond the hurt tha ruled his life. One more step and then another. Steps sh would take with him, and then he would see for himself th man she had always seen. ''How did you get a woman lik me?'' she asked as she slid her hand beneath his shirt. ''Jus luck, Mr. Slade. And the price of a bus ticket.''

''Have I told you I love you?''

''In this.'' She drew his note from beneath her pillow ''And with *Glory.*''

''*Glory.*'' There was regret on his face. ''You would'v been more beautiful.''

''The past is done. We have a future to make.''

''Do we?''

''Of course. I have the shop, and you were right, I'm ver good at it. You have your sculpture, and I was right there Since your magnificent presence at the show, your popu larity has tripled.''

''Are you teasing me just a little bit, tiger?''

''Of course, I am.'' Laughter eased her grief. Hunte would understand.

''Then you know our first priority is this.'' His mouth wa gentle on hers, saying words that were beyond him, prom ising dreams not yet dreamed, committing himself to Betl as he knew she was to him. Reluctantly, after a time, he dreᵥ away, just far enough to ask, ''Were you really going t leave me?''

"Only long enough for you to realize that you couldn't live without me." Her smile trembled. "I hoped."

"I can't, you know."

"You never have to."

"Then will you marry me?"

"I thought I had."

"The Cherokee rituals aren't elaborate, but..."

"You want to observe them. So do I." Tugging at his shaggy mane, she added, "That should make both parts of you mine."

"No ritual needed for that." He kissed her again, only managing to tear himself away when he felt the stirring of his body. "Christen threatened me with my life if I tired you." He made a move to leave, but Beth's arms twining about him held him fast.

"Stay with me. Hold me."

"I'll hold you," he murmured. "Now, tomorrow, for as long as it takes, until you're healed. And when you're stronger, we can make other babies. A whole tribe, if you want them."

"A tribe?"

"Give or take a few."

"I'd like that," she said, her voice drowsy.

"Then rest and heal," he whispered, drawing her close. She was his wounded tiger lady, but she was strong. Passion's day would come again, then she would be his glory.

* * * * *

SILHOUETTE® Desire™

COMING NEXT MONTH

#673 BABY ABOARD—Raye Morgan
Carson James was suave, charming and as far from fatherhood as a
man could get. Were Lisa Loring's enticing ways enough to lure him
into marriage...and a baby carriage?

#674 A GALLANT GENTLEMAN—Leslie Davis Guccione
Sailing instructor Kay McCormick had one rule for smooth sailing—
never get involved with club members! But then Jake Bishop and his
daughter guided her into the deep waters of love.

#675 HEART'S EASE—Ashley Summers
Valerie Hepburn's tragic past left her feeling undesirable and
unattractive. But could persistent businessman Christopher Wyatt
persuade Valerie to take a chance on living...and loving?

#676 LINDY AND THE LAW—Karen Leabo
Free-spirited Lindy Shapiro was always getting *into* and *out of*
trouble. But Sheriff Thad Halsey wasn't about to let this beauty
go...not before apprehending her heart.

#677 RED-HOT SATIN—Carole Buck
Hayley Jerome needed a fiancé fast—her mother was on her way to
meet him! Outrageous Nick O'Neill conned his way into playing Mr.
Wrong, but he felt very right.

#678 NOT A MARRYING MAN—Dixie Browning
When a silent five-year-old appeared on November's *Man of the
Month's* doorstep, secret agent Mac Ford had some questions. But
tracking down beautiful Banner Keaton only added to the mystery.

AVAILABLE NOW:

SILHOUETTE®
OFFICIAL SWEEPSTAKES
RULES

NO PURCHASE NECESSARY

1. To enter, complete an Official Entry Form or 3"× 5" index card by hand-printing, in plain block letters, your complete name, address, phone number and age, and mailing it to: Silhouette Fashion A Whole New You Sweepstakes, P.O. Box 621, Fort Erie, Ontario L2A 5X3.

   No responsibility is assumed for lost, late or misdirected mail. Entries must be sent separately with first class postage affixed, and be received no later than December 31, 1991 for eligibility.

2. Winners will be selected by D.L. Blair, Inc., an independent judging organization whose decisions are final, in random drawings to be held on January 30, 1992 in Blair, NE at 10:00 a.m. from among all eligible entries received.

3. The prizes to be awarded and their approximate retail values are as follows: Grand Prize — A brand-new Ford Explorer 4×4 plus a trip for two (2) to Hawaii, including round-trip air transportation, six (6) nights hotel accommodation, a $1,400 meal/spending money stipend and $2,000 cash toward a new fashion wardrobe (approximate value: $28,000) or $15,000 cash; two (2) Second Prizes — A trip to Hawaii, including round-trip air transportation, six (6) nights hotel accommodation, a $1,400 meal/spending money stipend and $2,000 cash toward a new fashion wardrobe (approximate value: $11,000) or $5,000 cash; three (3) Third Prizes — $2,000 cash toward a new fashion wardrobe. All prizes are valued in U.S. currency. Travel award air transportation is from the commercial airport nearest winner's home. Travel is subject to space and accommodation availability, and must be completed by June 30, 1993. Sweepstakes offer is open to residents of the U.S. and Canada who are 21 years of age or older as of December 31, 1991, except residents of Puerto Rico, employees and immediate family members of Torstar Corp., its affiliates, subsidiaries, and all agencies, entities and persons connected with the use, marketing, or conduct of this sweepstakes. All federal, state, provincial, municipal and local laws apply. Offer void wherever prohibited by law. Taxes and/or duties, applicable registration and licensing fees, are the sole responsibility of the winners. Any litigation within the province of Quebec respecting the conduct and awarding of a prize may be submitted to the Régie des loteries et courses du Québec. All prizes will be awarded; winners will be notified by mail. No substitution of prizes is permitted.

4. Potential winners must sign and return any required Affidavit of Eligibility/Release of Liability within 30 days of notification. In the event of noncompliance within this time period, the prize may be awarded to an alternate winner. Any prize or prize notification returned as undeliverable may result in the awarding of that prize to an alternate winner. By acceptance of their prize, winners consent to use of their names, photographs or their likenesses for purposes of advertising, trade and promotion on behalf of Torstar Corp. without further compensation. Canadian winners must correctly answer a time-limited arithmetical question in order to be awarded a prize.

5. For a list of winners (available after 3/31/92), send a separate stamped, self-addressed envelope to: Silhouette Fashion A Whole New You Sweepstakes, P.O. Box 4665, Blair, NE 68009.

PREMIUM OFFER TERMS

To receive your gift, complete the Offer Certificate according to directions. Be certain to enclose the required number of "Fashion A Whole New You" proofs of product purchase (which are found on the last page of every specially marked "Fashion A Whole New You" Silhouette or Harlequin romance novel). Requests must be received no later than December 31, 1991. Limit: four (4) gifts per name, family, group, organization or address. Items depicted are for illustrative purposes only and may not be exactly as shown. Please allow 6 to 8 weeks for receipt of order. Offer good while quantities of gifts last. In the event an ordered gift is no longer available, you will receive a free, previously unpublished Silhouette or Harlequin book for every proof of purchase you have submitted with your request, plus a refund of the postage and handling charge you have included. Offer good in the U.S. and Canada only.

SLFC-SWPR

SILHOUETTE® OFFICIAL SWEEPSTAKES ENTRY FORM

4-FCSDS-3

Complete and return this Entry Form immediately – the more entries you submit, the better your chances of winning!

- Entries must be received by **December 31, 1991**.
- A Random draw will take place on **January 30, 1992**.
- No purchase necessary.

Yes, I want to win a FASHION A WHOLE NEW YOU Sensuous and Adventurous prize from Silhouette:

Name _____ Telephone _____ Age _____

Address _____

City _____ Province _____ Postal Code _____

Return Entries to: Silhouette FASHION A WHOLE NEW YOU,
P.O. Box 621, Fort Erie, Ontario L2A 5X3   © 1991 Harlequin Enterprises Limited

PREMIUM OFFER

To receive your free gift, send us the required number of proofs-of-purchase from any specially marked FASHION A WHOLE NEW YOU Silhouette or Harlequin Book with the Offer Certificate properly completed, plus a check or money order (do not send cash) to cover postage and handling payable to Silhouette FASHION A WHOLE NEW YOU Offer. We will send you the specified gift.

OFFER CERTIFICATE

Item	A. SENSUAL DESIGNER VANITY BOX COLLECTION (set of 4) (Suggested Retail Price $60.00)	B. ADVENTUROUS TRAVEL COSMETIC CASE SET (set of 3) (Suggested Retail Price $25.00)
# of proofs-of-purchase	18	12
Postage and Handling	$4.00	$3.45
Check one	☐	☐

Name _____

Address _____

City _____ Province _____ Postal Code _____

Mail this certificate, designated number of proofs-of-purchase and check or money order for postage and handling to: Silhouette FASHION A WHOLE NEW YOU Gift Offer, P.O. Box 622, Fort Erie, Ontario L2A 5X3. Requests must be received by December 31, 1991.

ONE PROOF-OF-PURCHASE

4-FWCSD-3

To collect your fabulous free gift you must include the necessary number of proofs-of-purchase with a properly completed Offer Certificate.

© 1991 Harlequin Enterprises Limited

See previous page for details.